A SENSE OF GRATITUDE

Biren Banerjee

First published in 2021 by
Becomeshakespeare.com

One Point Six Technologies Pvt Ltd.119-123, 1st Floor,
Building J2, B - Wing, WadalaTruck Terminal, Wadala East,
Mumbai, Maharashtra, India, 400022.T:+91 8080226699

© ISBN - 978-93-5458-207-3

For my incredible Parents

Late Narendra C Banerjee
Late Jyotsna R Banerjee

To my lovely wife Shyamli

and my two excellent sons,

Vikram and Vishal

FOREWORD

I grew up in a house full of books. Since childhood, I have been an avid reader. My father, despite an extremely busy schedule, managed to read bedtime books to me and my brothers and sisters most evenings. My mother could recite and sing Rabindranath Tagore's poetry and songs by heart.

My wife is from a Marwari (Rajasthani) North Indian background and has always been keen to learn about Bengali culture – in particular my ancestors' story.

This book is not a biographical story of my ancestors. It is a simple story of my gratitude based partly on their lives, and an attempt to commemorate their lives in this book.

Having had a very busy career meant it was difficult to write this book. But at last I found the time, overcame my laziness, and sat down in one place to write it.

My sincere thanks and love to my wife Shyamli and my two sons Vikram and Vishal. My love and gratitude to my two superb daughters-in-law Lydia and Neha and my three grandchildren Asher, Rohan and Shona.

Last, but very much not least, my grateful thanks to Martin Booth for editing this book and making it readable.

I have to Thank hugely to few people in Mumbai for publishing - so all the staff of Become Shakespeare (becomeshakespeare.com) - particularly Miral Bheda and Trupti Sawardekar. I am also inundated for the support and help I received from Supriya Chakrabarty and Raghab Banerjee.

- Biren Banerjee
July 2021

WHERE THIS STORY HAPPENS

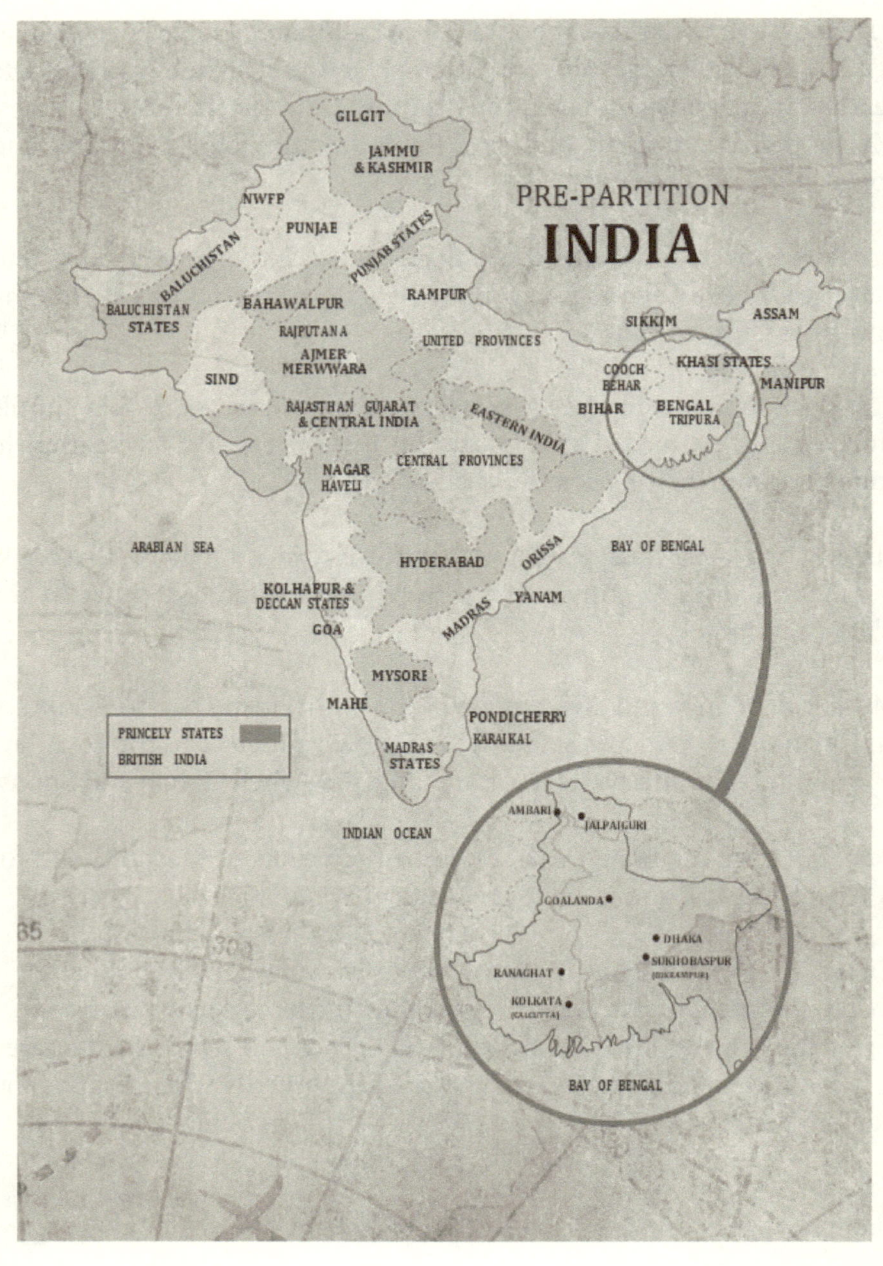

FAMILY TREE

Banerjee (Bandyopadhyay)
BINA BANERJEE
DHRUVA BANERJEE
ISHWAR BANERJEE
GOURI MUKHERJEE
APURVA BANERJEE
RADHA BANERJEE
BHUBAN BANERJEE
ADITYA BANERJEE
SARASWATI CHATTERJEE
SHARMILA GANGULY
SOUMITRA BANERJEE
ABHISHEK BANERJEE
ASHOK BANERJEE
TARINI MUKHERJEE

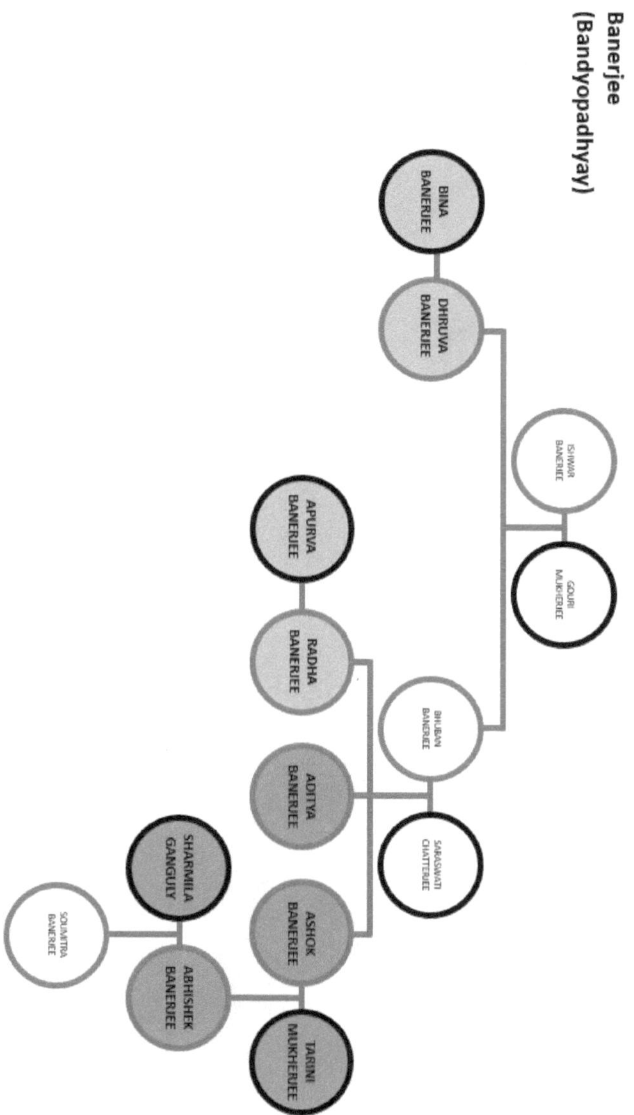

Mukherjee

NIRMAL MUKHERJEE
SEFALI CHATTERJEE
DEVIKA BHATTACHARYAY
RAJEN MUKHERJEE
PRATIMA MUKHERJEE
SHANKAR SANYAL
MALTI CHAKRABORTY
ANAND MUKHERJEE
LAXMI CHATTERJEE
JAYA LAHIRI
ANUP MUKHERJEE
AAKASH MUKHERJEE
GEETA BAGCHI
REKHA ROY
NARAYAN MUKHERJEE
TARINI MUKHERJEE
ASHOK BANERJEE
DEV KUMAR MUKHERJEE
ABHISHEK BANERJEE
SHARMILA GANGULY

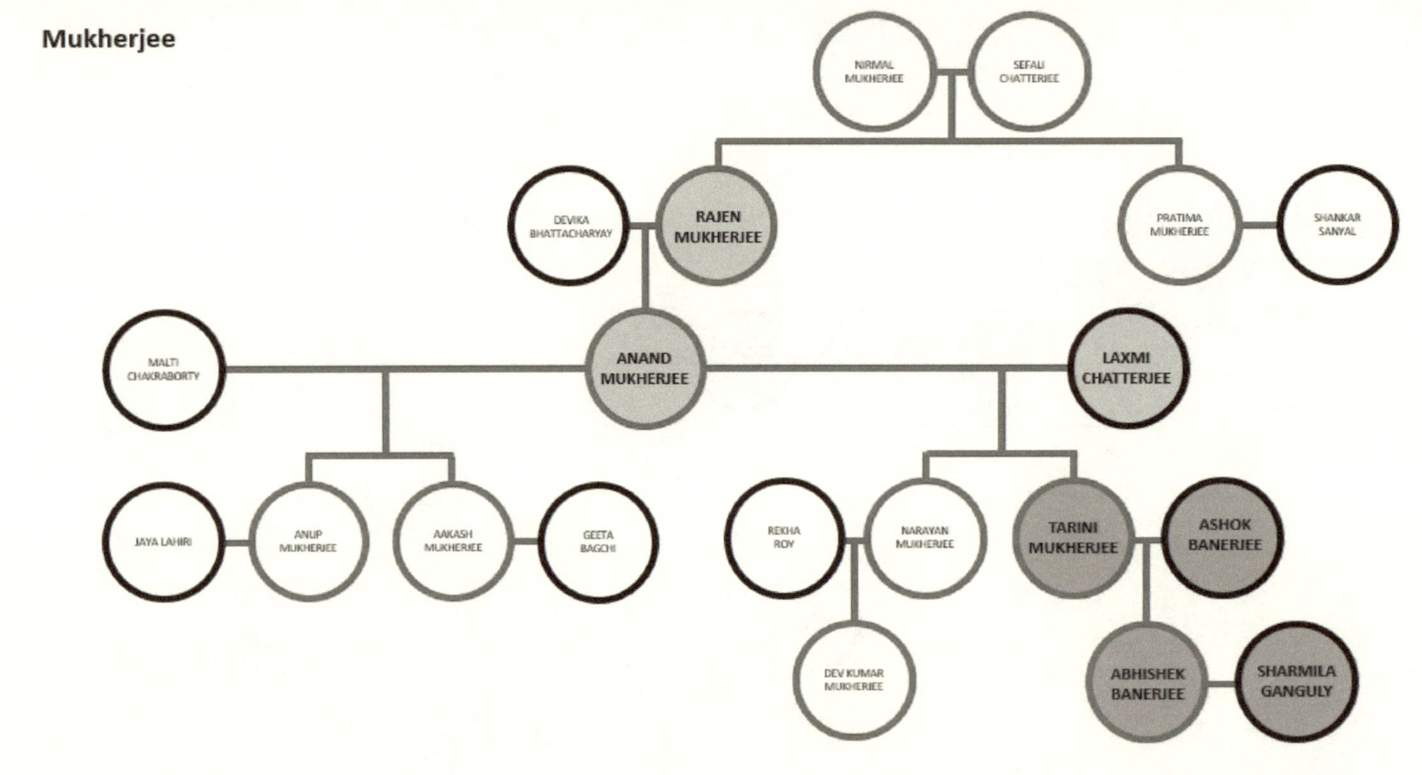

Ganguly

VIVEK GANGULY
RADHARANI DAS
MAMTA GANGULY
ABHISHEK BANERJEE
SHARMILA GANGULY
ANURADHA GANGULY
CHANDAN GANGULY

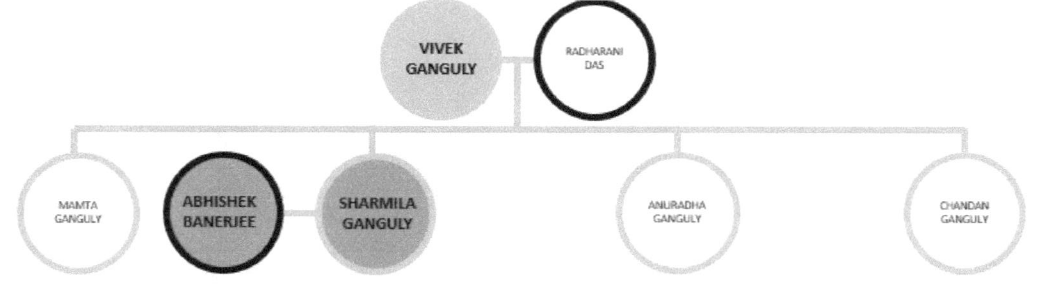

GLOSSARY OF INDIAN TERMS

Aarti – a Hindu religious ritual using a small fire

Almirah – a wardrobe or cupboard

Alta –a red dye applied to hands and feet for cosmetic reasons

Baarat – a groom's wedding procession

Babu – a respectful term of address to a man, sometimes added to his name

Bahu – daughter-in-law

Betel **nut** – traditionally chewed as a mouth freshener

Bhabhi - informal name for a sister-in-law

Bhai – brother

Bhagavad Gita – holy Hindu scripture– Krishna's advice to Arjun before a war

Biri – a home-made cigarette with dried tobacco wrapped around leaves of a special tree

Bodhu boron – ritual to welcome a wife to her husband's house

Bou bhat – festivities to welcome a new wife to her house, where the new wife serves rice to all family members and friends

Boudi – a female relative, usually the elder brother's wife

Cantonment – an area used, or previously used, as a military or police HQ

Castes – a division of Hindu society. The castes were Brahmin, Kayastha, Kshatriya, Vaishya and Shudra.

Chachi – aunt, father's younger brother's wife

Chaddar – a type of shawl

Choto maa – literally a "younger mother", father's second wife

Coolie – an unskilled labourer or porter

Dada – older brother

Dhoti – traditional male Indian dress similar to a sarong

Didi – respectful term of address to a familiar older woman

Diwali – the Hindu festival of lights

Durga Puja – a Hindu festival celebrating the victory of the goddess Durga over the demon king Mahishasura. A popular festival in Bengal.

Fatua – a cotton shirt

Ganesh Puja – a Hindu ritual to the god of success

Gayatri Mantra – a highly revered meditative chant

Ghatak – a matchmaker

Ghee – clarified butter

Gur – unrefined, solid sugar

Guru – a teacher or guide

Hate khori – ceremonial introduction to learning for small children

Hazak - a kerosene lamp with prism lenses to make the light even brighter

Hookah – an earthen pipe

Imam – a Muslim religious leader

Inshallah - Muslim expression, literally "If God wills it"

Ji – suffix added to a person's name implying respect

Kali Puja – a Hindu festival of the goddess Kali celebrating the triumph of good over evil

Kharam – wooden sandals

Khatiya - a traditional woven bed

Khichri – a dish of rice and lentils

Kurta – a long loose, collarless shirt

Lassi – drink made from yogurt or buttermilk

Lathi – a heavy walking stick

Laxmi Puja – a Hindu festival of the goddess of wealth

Mahabharata – an ancient Sanskrit epic. The main story revolves around two branches of a family - the Pandavas and Kauravas - who, in the Kurukshetra War, battle for the throne of Hastinapura.

Maidan – a large open space

Mali – a caste of people who traditionally worked as gardeners and florists

Namaste – respectful Indian greeting

Nawab – a provincial ruler

Neem stick – a special tree branch used for cleaning teeth

Om – chant that starts or concludes a mantra. In Hinduism, Om is one of the most important spiritual sounds. Om refers to Atman (soul, self within) and Brahman (ultimate reality, entirety of the universe, truth, divine, supreme spirit, cosmic principles, knowledge).

Paan leaves – traditionally chewed as a mouth freshener

Palki – a sedan chair

Pandal – a marquee

Pandit – local priest and matchmaker

Pathshala – a village primary school

Pati-patra – ceremony to confirm a marriage

Peon – a menial worker

Pice – a small coin, worth 1/64 of a rupee

Poori – a deep fat fried bread

Pradeep – a clay candle with oil

Punjabi –a tunic-like piece of clothing

Puja – an act of Hindu ritualworship

Raj – the British rule of India

Ramayana – an ancient Sanskrit epic text

Rasgulla – Indian sweet, a ball of curd cheese cooked in syrup

Roti – flat, round bread

Sahib – polite form of address for a man

Salaam alaikum - Formal Muslim greeting

Saraswati Puja – a Hindu festival to the goddess of knowledge and art

Sari – a long, traditional female garment

Shankh – a seashell that can be blown, like a conch, to produce sound

Shehnai – a musical instrument

Shloka - a poetic form used in Sanskrit

Shradh Puja – a Hindu ritual after death

Sindoor – orange-red powder worn on the forehead by married women

Sraddha - Hindu funeral ritual

Thakur ghar – a home temple

Thali – a metal plate

Tilak – a mark worn on the forehead on special occasions

Tulsi – a tree sacred to Hindus

Zamindar – a large land-owner

PART ONE

CHAPTER 1

The year was 1890. India was under British rule. A rule that had its origins in trade. The East India Company, which had been founded on New Year's Eve 1600, arrived in India in 1608 looking to trade in cotton, tea, spices and other commodities. It was only later that the Company seized power and effectively became the ruler of this vast, diverse and beautiful country. India became colonised, part of the growing British Empire.

Through the 1600s the Dutch, Danes, French and Portuguese all came to India and ruled small pockets of the country. But no nation took complete control of the administration of India like the British. They changed the transport system of the country, constructing railways, canals and bridges. The education system was also modernised through the Raj.

The British came at an interesting time in Indian history. The mighty Mughal Empire was crumbling and its last emperor, Bahadur Shah, was losing control of the vast nation when the British arrived in 1690 in a small village called Sutanuti, on the banks of the River Ganges. Sutanuti later merged with two other villages to become the city of Calcutta, now Kolkata.

Calcutta became the capital of Bengal. In 1757 it was ruled by a *Nawab* called Siraj ud-Daulah. The British helped his brother-in-law topple him and Siraj ud-Daulah was forced to leave the country in the middle of the night following the Battle of Plassey. This instability allowed the British to get a fairly easy foothold on business in India through the next *Nawab*, Mir Qasim.

The import and export business steadily grew ever more successful and eventually the British took over, ruling the country. Although there were some uprisings, most notably the Sepoy Mutiny in 1857, the British crushed them all with an iron fist. The sentiment that the British should quit India did not gain much momentum till the very late 1800s.

India is a very old civilisation. It is mostly a Hindu country. India has one of the world's oldest languages in Sanskrit and its oldest written epic novel, The *Mahabharata*. However, it has been ruled by various leaders over the years. The longest reign was that of the Mughals, who came from Samarkand, now Uzbekistan.

India was also the cradle of Buddhism, which at its peak was the religion of almost all of south-east Asia. India was also the birthplace of Jainism and of *Guru* Nanak, who founded Sikhism. Islam spread across the country during Aurangzeb's reign of the Mughal Empire, with most converts coming from Hinduism and Buddhism. Christianity was introduced by the British and other Europeans, notably the Portuguese. About 2% of modern Indians are practising Christians.

Once British rule started in Bengal, the prosperity of the area rose quickly. At one stage the GDP of Bengal was higher than many European countries'. Calcutta became the capital of the British Raj in India, so its anchorage, at Khidirpur, became very important. A huge amount of cargo used to come and go from this port, mainly to Europe and British destinations like Southampton and Liverpool.

Because of the economic boom, Calcutta underwent a complete makeover. Many roads, railway lines, bridges, schools and hospitals were built as Calcutta became the economic and cultural hub of India. Many of the big courts, sporting events and cultural events took place in Calcutta. It truly merited its title as capital of India.

Some 85 per cent of Indians worked in agriculture, but many young people started working in the civil service and new factories. The English language became compulsory in schools. Most of the executive posts in any service were held by British people. At one stage, 42,000 British people lived in Calcutta.

Bengal is full of rivers. It is dominated by the Ganges, but in different parts it has other names. In East Bengal it is called the Padma, in part of West Bengal it is the Hooghly. Bengal also has a tributary of the Brahmaputra, which comes from Assam. All of these rivers and tributaries join in the delta at the Bay of Bengal. All this makes Bengal a very fertile land that grows more than enough food to feed its population.

There are three main seasons – summer, winter and the rainy season. Summer can be very hot and some years at midday it can be difficult to go outside without the sun burning your face. The rainy season is wet, though not as much as in the neighbouring province of Assam. In some years, the monsoon can be terrible. It blows from the North and brings a huge amount of rainfall, raising the level of the Ganges, flooding many lowlands and uprooting many trees. Every year a few people die as a result.

That's why the three months of winter, and the very short autumn, is a time of celebration as the weather becomes calm. All the festivals take place during this time.

Bengal is essentially divided into two parts. The northern area stretches up to the foothills of the Himalayas, while the southern part is made up of the Ganges plane, one of the most fertile areas in the world. The Ganges river itself rises in the Himalayas and runs for nearly 1,700 miles through two large cities, Calcutta and Dhaka (Padma), before reaching the Bay of Bengal.

Dhaka, now the capital of Bangladesh, was a cultural hub, a beautiful city with many educational institutions. To travel from Dhaka to Calcutta you would either use the Ganges or the railways the British built.

Most of the houses were bungalows made of bamboo and mud, with a thatched roof. Every house would have many small rooms, with low doors and one small window for ventilation. Almost all houses used to have a small veranda and a central porch for people to gather. Often there would be a *Tulsi* tree, where ladies used to pray in the evening with lamps. Some people would have a *Thakur Ghar*, a room for worship.

Every house was surrounded by plenty of trees, mainly coconut, mango, banana and a local type of plum. Many homes would have a patch which the ladies of the house used to grow their chosen vegetables. Almost all the homes had a shed to house the family cows, which were very well looked after. There was a communal pond where people from nearby houses would bathe. This was how middle-class families lived, but landlords' houses would be much bigger and more affluent.

Cooking was done in a separate small kitchen, the domain of the ladies of the house. The oven was made of mud and fixed in the floor, though some houses had small clay ovens that could be taken out of the house. Cooking would start very early in the morning, having been planned the previous night by the most senior lady of the house.

Ladies would normally get up very early, before the men. They would bathe in the pond, change into a clean sari and go to the *puja* room in their house and worship for an hour or so. Some of the elders would stay longer to worship while the younger ones went to cut vegetables and grind herbs. The elder ladies would then join them and give instructions about what to do and how to cook.

Men would get up later. The most common breakfast was rice flakes (like cornflakes but white in colour) eaten with fresh milk from the house's own cow, accompanied by fruit juice from the local trees. Landless farmers would start work early, mainly in paddy fields. The sun would become very hot and in some months, by midday it would be unbearable, even though they would be wearing a bamboo hat for the heat.

After midday, some of the younger ladies of the house would bring lunch for the men. They would sit under a tree and have lunch with some water or coconut water, which is abundant in Bengal. After lunch the men would rest under the trees while the ladies would go back home. When the sun became less hot, the men would return to the fields.

But farm owners did not get their hands dirty. Their routine was different.

By evening, as darkness descended, everybody would pack up for home. Ladies would get ready for the men coming home, lighting the *pradeeps* everywhere around the house, including the central *Tulsi* tree.

Before coming home, the men would have a dip in the pond to clean up, and change clothes to freshen up. Then they would go to the *puja* to pray and sing hymns with the ladies. After the prayers it was time for dinner, where all the men and children in the family would sit on the floor on a small wooden platform and food was served by ladies. The talk would be about business and family issues. Only when the eldest members of the family had finished could everybody else leave. Then the ladies would eat and clear everything away before bedtime.

The staple food throughout India was rice and lentils. However, with Bengal being on the coast there was an abundance of seafood. Bengalis love a dish of rice and fish curry. In those days most people were vegetarian but, as an odd quirk of the time and location, fish was counted as vegetarian! The other weakness that all Bengalis have is a sweet tooth. Most of the sweets are made from cheese and sugar cane, usually from *gur*.

People dressed very simply. Men wore a *dhoti* and a *Fatua*, a type of shirt. And women used to wear *saris*.

Bengalis are generally happy people, they like to live a relaxed life and each week they regale hundreds of stories and sing hundreds of songs to whomever will listen.

The weather was reasonable. There are basically four seasons in Bengal. The summer could be extremely hot at midday and people used to stay at home after lunch and go out to work again in the late afternoon. The rainy season or monsoon could be very harsh. Some years it rained continuously for days, causing the river to break its banks and flood, making life miserable and often bringing outbreaks of cholera and typhoid.

The autumn was not too long but the weather allowed the men to work hard in the fields. Winter was the most pleasant part of the year. In the north of Bengal, it could snow. The whole country was full of vegetables and flowers and all the Hindu festivals are during the winter months - *Durga Puja, Kali Puja, Laxmi Puja and Diwali.*

Bengal had three religions: Hinduism, Islam and Buddhism. During the latter days of the Mughal Empire, many Hindus and Buddhists converted to Islam. When Sufi Islam came to Bengal, many more people were converted to Islam. The North and the West part were Hindu dominated, while the East and South were mostly Muslim..

Hindus had many castes: Brahmins, Kayasthas, Kshatriyas, Vaishyas and Shudras. This was a practice that dated back to the Sena Dynasty in Bengal in the 11th and 12th centuries. People were given a caste according to their occupation.

The caste groups lived together. There would be a Brahmin village where the upper caste, the teachers and the priests, used to live with their family. Then a village for Kayasthas, one for Kshatriyas, Vaishyas and Shudra. The lower *castes* were those who did menial jobs. Then there were Muslim villages. Although Hindus and Muslims mixed at work, they rarely socialised outside of that.

CHAPTER 2

This story starts in 1890 in a picturesque village called Sukhobaspur, located in a district of Bikrampur, which is about 40 miles from Dhaka.

Bikrampur was very famous in ancient times. The learned Dipankar, who was born there, was one of the first disciples of Buddha. He took Buddhism across South Asia to countries including Sri Lanka, Burma, Thailand and even Japan.

As with most of Bengal, the soil in Bikrampur was very fertile and rice was the main harvest. The harvest was once a year and, while the people were not very wealthy, they were self-sufficient. They used to cultivate fish in the ponds and every house had a small patch of land where they would grow vegetables for home use.

India was a feudal system. It had very wealthy land-owners, a few small land-owners and the poor landless farmers. Land-owners were known as *Zamindars*.

The biggest *Zamindar* in Bikrampur was Anand Mukherjee. He had inherited his land, which stretched as far as the eye could see, and was by all accounts a very rich man. Without modern accountancy practices and internet banking, we don't know exactly how much wealth he had – but he had plenty.

He had a large extended house in the middle of his land, with multiple rooms. The family had two separate kitchens, two store rooms and one large, elaborate temple. Outside were two tube-wells, with cowsheds on the banks of a large, well-stocked pond.

The centrepiece of the land was a grand old banyan tree. It was huge and mighty, with the characteristic aerial roots growing down from the branches like long braids.

The floor around the tree was kept very clean. In the evening, Mr

Mukherjee used to sit under the shade of the tree, with a cup of home-made juice, looking over his land. What a sight it was. A beautiful scene, especially as the sun set over the ponds and paddy fields, with the shadows of the mango trees and coconut trees creating a dancing ball over the water. Moonlit nights were also majestic, though you had to be careful going out at night because there was no electricity and no lights outside the houses.

At other times he would be joined by his cashier, who would sit in a small, flimsy stool next to the solid wooden chair. The village would also often congregate in a circle around him like a school fair. These would be times of lively discussion, talking about anything and everything. However, Anand *Babu* would always have the final say.

Mr Mukherjee was 56 or 57 years old. We are still 80 years from the introduction of birth certificates to India, so we cannot be entirely sure. He was a good-looking man. About six feet tall, with sharp features and dark, well oiled and parted hair. He had a long, almost Roman nose and large slanting eyes. His stature and mannerisms marked him out as a well-off man. Anand Mukherjee had two wives, which was not uncommon among wealthy landowners in those days.

His dress was simple; a *dhoti* made from cotton and a well-stitched Punjabi on top. Both were very white and fine. In winter he would wear a *Chaddar*, a type of shawl. This used to come to him from a special weaver in Shantipur. In the house he would wear wooden sandals, called *Kharam*. Outside he had a leather palm shoe. Sometimes he used a stick to walk around. He felt it gave him "*Zamindar* gravitas".

His daily routine was simple. In the morning he bathed outside the house, using both a dip in the pond and then the tube well with a bucket and hand soap. Before that he would clean his teeth with a *neem* stick which was common in those days. Mustard oil was lathered over his body, and coconut oil in his hair, before the pond dip. After bathing, he changed and went to his *thakur ghar* and recited from religious texts and the *Gita*. Then breakfast started. He would have fruit juice, depending on the season, then two *rotis*, some milk and some sweets called *gur*.

When his cashier Kanji *Babu* arrived, Mr Mukherjee would look at all the books and tell him who to give money, rice and lentils to, and how much. Kanji *Babu* would write it down. Mr Mukherjee would also tell him who to call in the office.

Then it was time to go to the villages. Mr Mukherjee would walk in front and Kanji *Babu* behind, carrying the umbrella over Mr Mukherjee's head. At the villages he would stop to talk to everyone; he knew the names of every single person there. They would discuss the crops, water and rainfall. Some could predict rain just by looking at the sky.

Mr Mukherjee was very experienced in agriculture and gave sage advice on matters such as the use of fertilisers. He would inspect the many big ponds he owned; he would ask the men who oversaw the pond how much they were feeding the fish, and other matters. By now the sun was getting hot, so he would go back to his office, where people would come to him with their problems.

After midday, when the sun was very hot, Mr Mukherjee would go home and lie on the veranda on a rug. A local massage man would come to give him a full body massage with mustard oil. After lying for up to an hour, he would go down to the pond, which was slightly warm by now, and swim a few lengths. It was a good thing the ladies did not use the pond at this time! After swimming he would sit under the tube-well while someone pumped water to rinse him off. Then he would change into clean clothes and stop at the temple for a short prayer before entering the kitchen, where food was waiting for him.

He was served food in a large *thali*, a metal plate, with many small pots. At the centre was a small hill of rice, with five different colourful and aromatic foods in different bowls around the rice. These could be lentils, fried aubergine, a vegetable curry, a fish curry and one sweet and sour plate. Mr Mukherjee would sit on a *pira*, a small stool, flanked by both his wives. The elder wife would normally serve the food while the younger used a hand fan which she moved from side to side to keep him cool. Mr Mukherjee always commented positively on the quality of food and cooking.

After lunch he would return to the tube well, this time to wash his hands. The young wife would stand with a hand towel for him. He would have some *Betel* nuts and paan leaves, a mouth freshener frowned upon nowadays but believed in 1890 to be good for digestion. Mr Mukherjee then went to one of his two bedrooms (one for each wife) for a short siesta to avoid the hottest part of the day.

After about an hour, with the clock showing just after 4pm, the courtyard had been transformed into a boardroom. The biggest chair was for Mr Mukherjee, who also had use of a foot stool. People began to arrive; there was a chair reserved for the village head man and one for the cashier. The boardroom table was large and round, organised in such a way that everyone could see and hear Mr Mukherjee.

Discussions covered subjects from personal to local to international. As is the way all round the world, on most days the idle chit-chat started with a comment on the weather. It would move on to rainfall, soil condition and what vegetables to grow.

Once these obligatory discussions were over, the group moved to more important issues, like family disputes. Mr Mukherjee was the ultimate judge and jury and people would accept his decisions.

A servant would pass round a hookah, an earthen pipe, to everyone for a puff or two. Discussions would last for some while but Mr Mukherjee would always call time before the moon was at its highest.

Every year there were many religious and agricultural festivals in the village. The biggest was *Durga Puja,* then *Kali Puja* and *Saraswati Puja.* Most were in the winter months which, while very cold, were mostly dry. There were plenty of flowers, fruit and vegetables. Organising the pujas was the big talking point of the evening meetings throughout the winter.

By eight o'clock, all the kerosene lamps were lit outside and inside. Mr Mukherjee would wash his hands and come to the kitchen, where the whole family would have dinner together before everybody went to their bedroom. Village life dictated that people went to bed early and woke up at dawn. Mr Mukherjee had two bedrooms so he would decide which to go but there was an unwritten rota and, because both wives got on very well, it was never a problem.

++++

Anand first got married when he was 18 or 19, in the early 1850s. Because he was the eldest child, as soon as he was mature enough his father decided it was time for Anand to marry and to start helping in the family business. So the matchmakers were called in.

These matchmakers were *pandits*, the local priests. They used to perform the pujas in the area, moving from family to family and village to village. So, they were the best link men to know whose boys and whose girls would be a good match. They would have bags full of suitable boys' and girls' pictures and horoscopes.

They would get a lot of presents, particularly from the girl's side, for arranging a suitable match. The *pandit* would go to a boy's house and show the girl's photograph and describe the attributes of the girl. These ranged from how fair the girl was, how long her hair was, and how sweet the girl looked. They sometimes oversold the girl's attributes to the boy's side.

At the first meeting, the *pandit* asked Anand's father, Rajen *Babu*: "Are you seriously thinking of giving Anand's marriage this winter? If so, I have got an excellent girl in mind."

This piqued Rajen's interest. "Oh yes?"

"She is from the next village. The family are Brahmins, as you are."

"Excellent."

"And the girl looks, I am not exaggerating, exactly like the goddess *Parvati*. I swear."

Rajen *Babu*'s response was swift and decisive. "If that is the case, let's make the arrangements. My brother-in-law and I can come and see the girl and negotiate the terms and conditions… provided what you say is true!"

The *pandit* said: "No worries. I am in their house next week for puja. I will organise the appointment then for early next month."

Rajen *Babu* said: "Sounds good. You have to give me at least two weeks' notice, so that I can organise a *palki*."

In due course, Rajen *Babu* was informed that they could come to visit the girl and have lunch. The meeting had to be during the day, because the absence of electricity meant there was no other way to see the girl.

When the day came, Shankar *Babu* (Rajen's brother-in-law) got ready with a new *dhoti* and Punjabi to go to Sanatanpur, the next village, about 20 miles away. They sat in the *palki*, were carried by six people and arrived at the village around midday. The *pandit* was sitting under a big banyan tree waiting for them.

The *pandit* said: "Welcome, sir. I have been waiting here for you since early morning. Everything is organised."

Rajen *Babu* asked: "What is the gentleman's name we are going to meet? I seem to have forgotten."

"He is called Keshab Chatterjee. He is a small land-owner."

The three short, squat men started walking to Keshab's house along open, bright and dusty village roads through beautiful scenery. Soon they spotted two gentlemen with folded arms standing outside a big bungalow.

The younger gentleman came forward and said: "I am Keshab Chatterjee and this is my brother. We are very grateful that you came all the way to see my daughter."

As soon as they arrived at the courtyard, a young man bought glasses of *lassi* for the guests. Keshab said: "That's my son." They brought out a few chairs in the courtyard and everyone took their seat. Then Keshab's wife came out, her face covered by a sari, and during a pleasant discussion invited them to her kitchen for lunch. In this situation the food was very important.

They had a five-course meal, all cooked by Keshab's wife, and it was delicious. Then they washed their hands and sat in the courtyard and listened to Keshab describe how he built the house, how many banana trees there were and what his plans were for further building. Shankar had to cut him off and say: "Before it gets too dark, we need to go back. We had better meet the dear girl, the reason we are here."

After a few minutes a girl, barely 16 years old, wearing a red sari and covered from head to toe, came in carrying in one hand a tray with some sweets on it. Her other arm was wrapped tightly around the arm of Keshab's sister-in-law, her aunt. The girl put the tray on the table. There were some *rasgullas* and sweet cheese.

Keshab *Babu* introduced her: "This is my only daughter, Lakshmi." The girl touched everybody's feet as a sign of respect and Keshab asked his daughter to sit on the chair. It was a small, round table, around which were Rajen *Babu* and Shankar *Babu* on one side, with Keshab *Babu* and his his brother on the other, with Lakshmi sitting on a small chair. Behind her, her aunt remained standing.

Rajen *Babu* asked: "What's your name?"

The girl whispered, "Lakshmi Rani Chatterjee."

Rajen asked: "How old are you?"

"Just crossed 16."

"Can you read and write?"

Lakshmi said: "Yes. I have been to school and I can read and write."

Shankar *Babu* asked: "Can you cook?"

Lakshmi said: "Yes, but only a few things which my mum taught me."

The aunt quickly interjected: "Lakshmi can sing very well. Do you want her to sing?"

Rajen *Babu* started to say: "No, not really," but before he could finish Shankar said: "Yes, we would love to, why not?"

So, although Keshab *Babu* did not like it, they brought out a harmonium. There was no choice for Lakshmi.

She sang a Rajanikant devotional song and Rajen *Babu* said: "That was excellent."

Keshab said: "If you permit, can we let Lakshmi go? She is only 16."

"Of course," said Rajen *Babu*. Lakshmi touched everyone's feet again and, holding her aunt's hand, slowly disappeared.

Rajen *Babu* asked Keshab: "Can you give us two minutes to discuss?"

"Of course," said Keshab.

Rajen *Babu* pulled his chair close to Shankar's. Keeping his head down he whispered: "What do you think of the girl?"

Shankar said: "I like the girl. She will be a good wife."

So Rajen *Babu* said to Keshab: "We like your daughter. I will be happy to organise the marriage, but on two conditions. One is horoscopes – they have to match. We believe in that."

Keshab said: "Pandit-ji has already looked at both the horoscopes and he thinks they are a perfect match."

Rajen said: "That's fine then. The second point is, I am a big land-owner. I don't want to put any pressure on you for dowry, but I want a good marriage from your side for my son."

Keshab, his hands folded, said: "I have got a small land holding and a few ponds. And for the marriage I am happy to give two ponds and five acres of land to your son."

Shankar asked: "What about gold?"

Keshab, his hands still folded, said: "My wife has a reasonable amount of gold which Lakshmi will inherit."

Rajen *Babu*: "In that case, from my side you can take it as agreed."

Keshab held Rajen's hands and said: "It will be an honour for my daughter to be daughter-in-law in your *Zamindar's* family."

Rajen said: "In that case I will organise a date for *Pati-Patra* and a party afterwards. The other thing is, as you know a lot of people work for me and they would like to attend the marriage. So at least 100 people will come in Baraat."

Keshab said "I have only one daughter, so I will do whatever I can."

So, the marriage date was fixed after *pati-patra*. It was on a full moon day.

The baraat came from different villages, so they were given different houses to stay in at the girl's village because there were no other accommodation available. It was a huge undertaking on the girl's side. The boy's party came in a procession with a musical band and there was a lot of dancing before they entered the main *pandal*, where the main rituals took place. The groom was welcomed by the ladies with *tilak* and rituals.

The priest started the marriage by performing a *Ganesh Puja* and then put the fire on to start the main marriage rituals. Now the bride was brought in by her brothers, wearing a sari and with her face covered by a veil or *Betel* leaf. At this stage the bride was not supposed to see the groom's face. All the family and friends stood around the bride and groom while the priest kept chanting the holy words. Then the bride and the groom went around the fire and took their vows to look after each other.

While this was going on, the guests kept arriving and they were taken to the dining area and fed a huge amount of food and sweets. Meanwhile, in a small outside tent, a flautist and percussionist played happy music. On the day of the marriage, the couple fasted until the ceremony was over and they had taken the blessing of family and friends. They were then taken into the house for food, but outside the festivities and eating went on until early morning.

Rajen *Babu* and his baraat group were kept in a big schoolhouse. In those days female relatives and friends never came to a marriage, so all the guests were male.

There was a pond outside the school. On the marriage day, everybody had a pleasant swim before getting dressed up. Keshab *Babu* and his family arrived and all had breakfast in the school dining room, with *roti* and fried aubergines and some home-made sweets. They wanted to walk around the village to see how beautiful it was. Keshab *Babu* had other things to do, so his brother took them round.

Keshab ran home and spoke to his wife, Rani, who was keeping everything under control. He went to the fisherman, who promised to catch some good fish for lunch for their guests. It was decided they would have rice with lentils, and some fish and sweets.

While this was going on, Anand and Lakshmi had to go through some post-marriage rituals with the ladies. When Anand woke up, he couldn't find his shoes. They had been hidden by Lakshmi's friends and, as common custom dictates, Anand gave money to all of them. Lakshmi got a lot of presents. One of her cousins was busy packing all her presents because the bride and groom would be going back after lunch.

After everybody had lunch, Rajen *Babu* looked at his watch and told Shankar: "It's high time we start getting ready to go back, because it will get dark soon." Shankar went around to tell everybody that at five o'clock they would be leaving for home and they should be ready and waiting outside the school. But as Lakshmi's departure time came closer, the house became very quiet. It was a big moment for everyone that Lakshmi would leave her parents' house and go to a new home where she did not know anybody.

At five o'clock, lots of *palkis* arrived. One was packed with Lakshmi's clothes and presents. It was only a few miles to Anand's house, so all the men started getting into the allocated *palkis*. At last Anand came out with Lakshmi with the marriage knot in place. Lakshmi was holding her mum and crying profusely. Both the mother and aunt were still giving her advice on how to behave in the in-laws' house. Anand and Lakshmi, in the midst of the emotion, touched the feet of all the elders.

Some ladies were blowing *Shankh* and Lakshmi now had to throw some rice over her head in her father's house. It was an old ritual before entering her *palki*. She was inconsolable. Anand tried to help her to sit in the *palki* and the procession of *palkis* slowly started going towards Anand's village, leaving behind a picturesque village in mourning. The sun was still high but it was red, and it was going down. Rajen *Babu* felt everything had gone as planned and they would reach home before sunset. In the evening, Anand and Lakshmi, with all the other baraat members, arrived outside the house.

There was a huge number of women waiting at the gate with candles, flowers and garlands to welcome the newly-weds to their new house. Anand and Lakshmi approached the main gate slowly and were welcomed by all the ladies of the house.

Keshab was consoling his wife at home, saying: "We have done whatever we could do, we have a good son-in-law and I am sure Lakshmi will be very happy."

Once in his house, Anand left his new wife to the ladies and went for a chat with his dad and his friends about the upcoming *Bou bhat* . At this event, the bride would serve rice to all the elders of the family, followed by a big feast.

On the other side Lakshmi was taken by the ladies of the house for the *Bodhu boron*. She had to walk on a new sari after dipping her feet in *alta*. She was then taken to the kitchen to watch how milk is boiled. This is an old ritual. Next, she went to the puja room to take blessings from all the gods and goddesses. She was taken to her bedroom, which was decorated very well. There were flowers in every corner and a big bouquet in the middle of bed.

Lakshmi did exactly what she was told by her new in-laws. She also was told to be prepared for the following day, which is when a newly married *Bahu* would serve rice to all the elders. Her father and relatives would come for the big feast in the evening. So a small *pandal* would be built outside the house and there were two decorated chairs for Anand and Lakshmi to sit. All the guests would be introduced to the new bride and give them blessings and presents.

The following morning, Lakshmi woke up early. The ladies of the house took her to get ready for the day. The morning part was among family and went very well. But the evening was slightly daunting for Lakshmi. She had to sit in a big chair wearing new clothes with a long veil and had to get up and down to bow to all the family and friends. Anand's cousin sister was sitting next to her introducing everybody and also keeping a list of all the presents and who gave them.

Lakshmi was very quiet and calm, but it was a long day and she was feeling very tired. However, she continued to do whatever she was told and the only time she was excited was when she saw her father Keshab come to give his blessings. There were a few tears again in the evening when Lakshmi's family from her father's side had to leave. It was very emotionally draining for Lakshmi.

As it grew late, the local people slowly started departing. The lights were gradually switched off. Anand and Lakshmi had their first joint dinner together but Lakshmi could hardly eat. She could hardly keep her eyes open. She was just 16 and simply wanted to sleep. The ladies of the family took Lakshmi to her specially decorated and perfumed bedroom to start her first day of married life.

Anand and Lakshmi's family life started very pleasantly. Because they were very well off, Rajen *Babu* decided to extend the house so that Lakshmi could have a bigger bedroom and a separate toilet.

Things were quite regimental, which was not like her unmarried life. She had to maintain all the norms of her in-laws' family. She hated having to get up early in the morning before sunrise, but she got used to it. The routine was to get showered, changed and ready with her mother-in-law and to wear a fresh, clean sari every morning, with no make-up allowed.

She would head to the kitchen, which was full of female servants. Men were not allowed. Devika, Lakshmi's mother-in-law, was in charge. She was an overweight lady in her fifties with a formidable personality – nobody dared to contradict anything she said. She would decide the breakfast menu and she would give Lakshmi two glasses of milk with a spoonful of sugar, one for Rajen *Babu* and the other for Anand.

Milk was delivered early in the morning from their own cow shed. They had at least six cows, sometimes eight, so they had buckets full of milk. Half the family were vegetarian, so milk was used to make curds, cottage cheese and sweets. It was Lakshmi's first job to give milk to her father-in-law and her husband. Although Anand was very slow in the morning, he would have a glass of water first before the milk. It was then his turn to go to the pond and, after his swim, he would put some oil on his head and get ready, wearing a clean *dhoti* and Punjabi.

Next it was Rajen *Babu*'s turn. He would have a shower and get ready. Anand would be waiting for his father to turn up in the dining room for breakfast, which was served mainly by Lakshmi, but with Devika supervising everything.

At about nine in the morning, Anand was ready with his notebook and umbrella, and the cashier *Babu* would turn up. They would wait for Rajen *Babu* to come. He would take an extra half an hour they would then walk to their office. All the ladies, including Devika and Lakshmi, would be standing on the veranda.

The office was only a few hundred yards away, along earthen roads. It was in a building made of wood, bamboos and mud, with a thatched roof. The office was a big one. On the outside veranda there were a lot of mats for people to sit on and there was a small table where the cashier *Babu* sat, with a *peon* next to him on a small stool.

Inside was a big room, which was Rajen *Babu*'s office. This was decorated very well, with lots of pictures of his ancestors and a table and chair for Rajen *Babu*. Behind them were bookshelves and a small bed, where Rajen *Babu* used to rest a bit during his office hours. There was a small office next to it with a communicating door which was built for Anand.

The cashier *Babu* was a very polite, down-to-earth man who would do whatever Rajen *Babu* told him. He kept all the transactions in big red books and knew everybody in the village. The *peon* was a Muslim man called Abdul Maheed. He was a landless farmer and a Muslim. Because he had multiple health issues, he couldn't work in the field, so Rajen *Babu* appointed him as his *peon*. His job was to help cashier *Babu* and run around to call people Rajen *Babu* summoned. Abdul used to carry a stick and he had a weird sense of humour.

Rajen had recently had a health scare. He started getting recurrent chest pain after walking only a few yards, so he consulted a local homeopath and one in the city. Both suggested he should take things easy and give more responsibilities to Anand.

Devika insisted that Rajen should heed the medical advice and let Anand run the business while he supervised. But Rajen felt Anand was not mature enough yet. However, he eventually started getting Anand more involved in the business.

Each morning, upon arrival at the office, lots of farmers used to wait for advice and help from Rajen. One might need some money for his daughter's marriage, another had had no crop this year because of drought, while a third would need a loan for his wife's treatment. Rajen started to get Anand involved in deciding how much to give, and cashier *Babu* was also giving some training to Anand.

At lunch time, the food came from home for everybody in the office, with some special food for Rajen *Babu*. Anand, being newly married, would have liked to go home but Rajen *Babu* was very strict about work.

After lunch Rajen *Babu* would lie down for a couple of hours with his newspaper, while Anand and Abdul would go around the farm and the ponds to see how things were going. As the sun started getting too hot, after an hour or so, Anand and cashier *Babu* would come back. Abdul would give them a glass of lemon water with sugar.

At about four o'clock, Rajen *Babu* would call everybody into the office and ask what they had inspected so far. He might decide to go to the mango plant and go home from there. At the mango plant he would ask how many weeks it would be before the mangoes were ripe and when they planned to pick them. Abdul *Babu* would give him some cash and write it down in his book.

Then Rajen would walk past the pond, asking the men there to show the size of the fish. They would throw the net and bring a jumping fish to Rajen *Babu*. He might say: "It's not good enough. Give them some more food. I want this fish to double in size in two months."

The walk home from there was about two miles, and all the way Abdul would hold the umbrella over Rajen *Babu*'s head, with Anand walking one step behind. By six o'clock, when it was dusk, Rajen would call it a day, say goodbye to everybody and go to his room.

In the evening it would get dark very quickly because there was no electricity. Some well-off houses like Rajen *Babu*'s had lanterns and *hazak* lamps, which gave off light from pressurising a kerosene oil pot. They had a piston where you could pressurise the kerosene oil, while at the top there was a burner where you put the fire. There are some prism glasses around this fire which reflects and makes it very bright. You had to be very careful when using *hazak* lamps inside the house because if the pressure was raised too high, the light could burst.

Rajen *Babu*'s health was now not at its best. Not only was he getting chest pains but he was also becoming breathless. He was giving more and more responsibility to Anand and in the evening time he came home much earlier and would sit on a stool. One of the servants would wash his feet and Devika would take him to his room so he could rest for some time.

He would come out of the room late in the evening to sit in his usual chair in the courtyard, keeping his feet up, while Anand and all the village elders sat around him and one of the servants would make a *hookah*.

Because he was very liberal man who was both wealthy and respected, everybody and anybody would turn up and ask Rajen *Babu* to mediate in their problems. One man might say daughter was getting married, but the boy's side was asking for 10 grams of gold. Rajen *Babu* would ask: "Who is the boy's father? I will talk to him. I am sure he will accept it if I ask him."

While this was going on outside, Devika and Lakshmi, with the maidservants, would be preparing the evening meal. In these meetings Anand had very little to do but he always attended it to see how his dad solved every villager's problem.

Lakshmi would come out with her veil on and say: "*Babu-ji*, food is ready." Rajen would tell everybody to disperse. Then, he and Anand washed their hands, sat on small stools and food was served. It's a Hindu tradition that, before they start eating, they will keep food in five small pieces for their devoted Gods, then put water on that and then start eating. Evening meal used to be five courses, with rice being the staple. Fish was eaten more or less every night, but no meat was eaten in Mr Mukherjee's house.

There were two kerosene lamps on both sides of their copper plates and Lakshmi would serve food while Devika sat on another stool and supervised. After both the men had eaten and left the dining room, the wives and the ladies would sit and eat together and discuss the menu for lunch for the next day. By now Rajen and Anand had both gone to their respected bedrooms and the ladies washed all the utensils, cleaned the room and went to their own bedroom with a glass of water for their husbands.

Life was moving on very well in the Mukherjee family and their economy was booming. But one year in the early 1850s, the monsoon was horrific. It rained for months, all the rivers flooded and half the houses were under water. Even though the Mukherjee house was on higher ground, the water was waist-high in some places.

Rice, the main crop, lentils and most of the wheat were destroyed. Food shortages became extreme, the flood water took a long time to recede and there was a cholera outbreak in the village. But the Mukherjees were lucky, they had a huge stock of food inside their storage room.

People started queuing up for a small bit of rice and vegetables. The Mukherjees were very generous people and they tried their best to look after the villagers. But large numbers started dying, with nobody to cremate or bury them.

Anand became very involved with the flood relief project. He went from place to place to help people. Rajen *Babu*, however, became very depressed and unwell. He lost a lot of weight and started getting breathless. Anand went to town and got the best doctor and his assistant in a *palki* to visit their house to see Rajen. He said to the doctor: "Do whatever is required to make my father better."

In those days all doctors were trained in homeopathy. The doctor came and charged a lot of money for many bottles of medicine, while also arranging for a man to give Rajen a chest massage twice a day. But Rajen was still struggling. He kept telling Anand: "Maybe the diagnosis is not right."

Anand tried his best. He got another top doctor, from the city of Dhaka. This doctor said Rajen's heart was failing and he changed all his medication. However, early one morning Rajen suffered severe chest pain and died.

Rajen was cremated according to Hindu ritual. The fire was lit by his only son, Anand, who followed all the rituals. He went about in bare feet wearing only a *dhoti* and shawl, not shaving, not putting oil on his body and hair, and reading the *Gita* five times a day. On the 11th day after Rajen's death he invited all the local people and performed a *Shradh Puja*, praying for the soul of his deceased father and asking for peace to be on him. He kept a black and white photo of his dad, decorated it with garlands and put it on the table. Everybody who came bowed down and touched the feet of the picture. Lots of people cried inconsolably.

Devika, as a Hindu widow, took all her ornaments off. She had to cut her hair short, and wore only a white sari and became completely vegetarian, as the religion dictates.

Anand suddenly grew up in stature and responsibility. He became the Mr Mukherjee, the *Zamindar*. Now he was the man with all the duties of running the business. His father had groomed him for this. Anand also started talking, behaving and walking like his dad.

The flood slowly receded. Luckily, famine had been averted and Anand could see bright light at the end of the tunnel. After a year, he and Lakshmi's first daughter was born, a beautiful little girl.

Anand wanted to be sure the delivery went well, so, he got the best midwife and kept her at home during the last trimester of pregnancy. His daughter was given the name Tarini.

CHAPTER 3

Life went on in a very smooth, orderly fashion. Anand's business was doing well, and he started buying more agricultural land and a lot of gold as jewellery and an investment for Lakshmi. Tarini was growing up and when she was three, she got a brother called Narayan. Tarini was very good looking and fair skinned, something that was considered an asset in those days. Narayan had a darker complexion but was athletic and sociable.

Lakshmi had some help to look after the two toddlers and they had lots of toys to play with. When Tarini was five, she was given home tutoring in Sanskrit and Bengali. Sanskrit is one of the oldest languages of the world, also called *Devanagari* because all the Gods' recitals and songs were initially sung in this language. Indian civilisation has been depicted through Sanskrit from ancient times. A difficult language, it was the source for many regional dialects. Hindi and Bengali are two important derivatives from Sanskrit.

Village life was pretty pleasant while growing up. There were no main or big roads, just small paths. The houses were very spread out. Everybody used to know each other by their parents' name. There was lots of greenery, with flowers everywhere and, in the middle, endless paddy fields. Bengal is in the delta of the Bay of Bengal and the earth is very fertile. There were ponds everywhere. On a nice, dry day, the village looked like a picture postcard. Life here was very peaceful and gentle.

There were lots of sports. The boys used to play kabaddi, a very physical sport played by six players on each side. The girls used to be busy helping their mothers and used to play only around the house and courtyard. The village girls used to stick together wherever they went.

Boys used to wear all cotton clothes, usually a *dhoti* with a type of T-shirt called a *Fatua*. The girls, from a young age, used to wear short saris.

Tarini and Narayan were growing up. Tarini was learning all that the girls used to learn those days: knitting, making jumpers, sewing. Narayan, on the other hand, showed a keen interest in football and swimming and he became one of the leaders among his friends. The older people used to like Narayan because of his manners and nature. Lakshmi used to keep a very close eye on Tarini as, with all her friends, Tarini was growing up and learning all the Puja and rituals on which Lakshmi was very keen.

Durga Puja was a huge occasion in the village. It used to run for seven days. Schools were closed. The boys and girls were free. Anand was not only the biggest donor for the puja, he was also the president of the puja. They started bringing all the deities from different parts of Calcutta via boat along the Ganges.

The village ladies used to decorate the temple and the deities. This is the festival to make good win over evil. Tarini became very much involved with her mother and her friends in making clothes and ornaments for the deities. They used to get up early in the morning and the work would go on till late evening.

During the festival, everybody used to get new clothes. There was a lot of music and drums were played. Narayan was very busy dancing with fire during the puja. Everybody used to look forward to this festival and after this was finished, *Laxmi Puja*, another big festival, took place. It was a joyous occasion with lots of food, dancing and singing.

Anand had extended the house so that Tarini and Narayan both had their own bedrooms. Now Tarini was allowed to dress like a grown-up. For festivals like *Diwali* she was allowed to put alta on her hands and feet. Tarini learned to read and write fluently and could sing devotional songs with the harmonium.

By the time Tarini was 16 she was considered a very attractive woman. Although her movements were restricted, wherever she went people would enquire about her, which was embarrassing but also flattering for Tarini.

The *pandit* who performed the puja also carried out matchmaking in his spare time. He was also known as the *Ghatak* for this reason. The *pandit* told Anand *Babu*: "You have got a beautiful young daughter and she is also very talented. If you are keen or interested in her matrimony, I know a bright boy in the next village."

Anand *Babu* said to the *pandit*: "No, she is too young to get married yet. I want her to get some more education before marriage."

Ghatak Babu said: "In that case I will talk to you about Tarini in a few months' time."

About a year later, *Ghatak Babu* returned and said: "I have another proposal for you to consider, Anand *Babu*. I know a poor Brahmin guy in a faraway village. He is struggling to survive himself and his wife died some years ago.

"But he has a young daughter of 25. I will not lie to you. She is not good looking; thus it has become impossible to find a suitable boy for her."

Anand *Babu* said: "Why you are telling me all this?"

Ghatak said: "That poor man and the daughter need some help from people like you."

Anand said: "I don't know how I can help."

Ghatak Babu said: "There are a lot of wealthy *Zamindars* who have got two wives. If you don't mind, you could marry this young girl and save both the father and the daughter from starvation and death."

Anand *Babu* said: "No, I can't do that."

Ghatak said: "Can you think about it? It will be a great help. Without your support they would be destitute."

Anand *Babu* was quiet for a long time, then said: "OK, give me time to think it through and let me talk to Lakshmi. Come back in a couple of weeks' time."

Anand was very quiet and kept himself to himself as he pondered on what the *Ghatak* said. Lakshmi realised something was not right and bothering Anand. "What's the matter?" she asked. "Can I help?"

She thought it might be something related to business. But when Anand told her that he'd got a proposal to get married a second time to a poor man's daughter who was only 25, Lakshmi couldn't believe her ears. It felt as if her heart more or less stopped.

She said: "How do you propose to marry a girl so young?" She was completely against the idea. The discussion finished abruptly.

A few days passed, and Lakshmi realised that Anand was getting upset and depressed. So she relented and said: "If that's what you want to do, it's fine."

Anand decided not to have any fuss or festivities, just a simple ceremony. Lakshmi called Tarini and Narayan and told them that to help a family their father was planning to marry again and they should not make any fuss, but accept the new wife as their *Choto maa*.

So, on a summer afternoon Anand went with a priest and a *Ghatak* and married this girl and brought her home. Malati became the *Choto maa* in the house. Anand organised a job for her father on the land and a small hut for him to live in.

The Mukherjee family was completely reorganised. Now there were two bedrooms, one for Lakshmi and the other for Malati. Somehow Lakshmi started liking the girl and told her to call her *"didi"*. Although Lakshmi remained the main anchor of the house, Anand started sharing bedrooms with two different wives, "bara bou" and "choto bou".

Malati's father had virtually no possessions. Anand organised all his clothing and food and gave him a light job, and also gave him the responsibility to look after the temple and the deities. Lakshmi was still in charge, walking around the house with a large bunch of keys tied to the end of her sari, telling people what to do. Malati started walking one step behind her and people were surprised how well they got on. Although in those days, for a *Zamindar* to have two or even more wives was not unusual.

Lakshmi's bedroom was very simple. It was a large room with a big bed in the middle with a nice soft mattress and a quilt on top. There were two big *almirahs* full of Lakshmi's clothes. There was a box where Lakshmi used to keep all her jewelleries. And there was another *almirah* for Anand's clothes.

In contrast, Malati's bedroom was small and she had a mirror dressing table because she liked dressing up. She had a few deities' pictures and two small wooden boxes which she used to keep under the bed. Lakshmi was sharing her husband with a younger girl, but she was still in control.

After Malati's bedroom the house became L-shaped. There was a large room called *Thakur Ghar* or temple with all the deities: Radha Krishna, Laxmi and Kali were there. There were also some puja books. The gardener used to bring large number of flowers every morning for the puja. In the past Lakshmi used to do all the dressing of deities, but now she gave some responsibilities to Malati. The room smell like sandalwood. The next two rooms were Tarini's and Narayan's.

The morning briefing had changed. Where Lakshmi used to give instructions to everybody, now Malati also came to the kitchen and they decided what would be the menu for breakfast, lunch and dinner and who will do what. Every morning after breakfast Lakshmi did puja for an hour, during which nobody dared to disturb her.

Tarini and Narayan were told that they should read loudly. This way, they could hear what they were reading, and everybody would know they were studying.

The typical day in the Mukherjee family was like this. It would start slowly, with Anand having tea in his bed, then reading the monthly newspaper or the gazette and having his breakfast after getting ready. Then he would get ready to go to work. He had employed many more people with more responsibilities, so his workload had reduced quite considerably. Because of that he had picked up a hobby of pigeon shooting. The local collector was very keen on that, so Anand bought a few guns and whenever he had spare time he went out to shoot pigeons. An Englishman had come to the local town and, although language was an issue, he got on well with Anand.

Time moved on slowly and well. In two consecutive years Malati had two sons. Lakshmi, being like an elder sister, looked after Malati very well. Anand was in his mid-fifties with Tarini coming up to 18 and Narayan about 14. His other two sons, Anup and Aakash, were very small. But because of Lakshmi's guidance they tended to run a nice show.

As Tarini approached 18 she was very attractive and had finished her home schooling completely. Anand felt it was high time to call the *Ghatak*. He came to the Mukherjees' house every week, bringing pictures of suitable boys with their horoscopes and their prospects. But Lakshmi and Malati both became very fussy. They couldn't choose any of the boys the *pandit* brought. Anand *Babu* was getting very impatient and annoyed with both wives and kept asking what they were looking for.

After a month or so the *pandit* came back with a picture of tall young man. He was dark and had a moustache with very sharp features. The *pandit* said: "This guy has a brother and a sister. The boy in question is 26 and passed his matriculation exam from the University of Calcutta and already has a manager's job."

Lakshmi and Tarini both felt this boy was very handsome and educated; even though he was a bit dark, he was the boy.

His name was Ashok. His full name was Ashok Chandra Bandyopadhyay. He was a Bengali Brahmin of the highest caste called Shandilya, where Lord Krishna was born.

PART TWO

CHAPTER 4

In Sanskrit, Bandyopadhyay means "most venerable teacher or priest". Because colonial Englishmen found it a bit of a tongue twister, they shortened it to Banerjee, which became common usage. Along with the Mukherjees, Chatterjees, Bhattacharjees and Gangulys, the Banerjees formed the Brahmins, the highest tier of the traditional caste system.

It was Lakshman Sen who started the caste system in ancient times. He divided people into four main *castes* according to their profession: Brahmin, Kayasths, Kshatriya and Vaishya. The rest were lower caste.

Ashok was the eldest of three siblings. He had a sister who was about 20, called Radha, and a 14 year old brother called Aditya.

Ashok's parents had died when all three children were pretty young. There was a smallpox outbreak in eastern India, which wiped out millions of people and killed many young men and women. So the three children became orphans very young. One of their aunts and uncles used to give them parental support but it was difficult.

But by the grace of God, they had their own little mud house, a small holding of land and two small ponds. Life was hard but manageable. Ashok's uncle, Dhruva, owned a large amount of land, which he used to farm, and he also farmed the land which belonged to Ashok. He was a very honest and decent man who made sure there was food on the table for these three kids.

He told Ashok: "You have two choices. You can give up your education and join me in farming, because I have no children. I will give your share. The other option is that I will farm all the land, yours and mine, and share between us and I will make sure you get enough to survive." Ashok agreed with his uncle that he would continue his education and his uncle would do the farming. Whatever was required, his uncle would look after that.

Ashok's mind was clear. Now he could pursue his education and not worry about his brother and sister. Ashok was studying very hard because he was planning to sit the matriculation exam. Studying in the evening was not easy because there was no electricity. He had to study with a kerosene lamp – and the price of kerosene was going up every month because of British Government policy. Also, to get kerosene you had to go to the main town, which was time-consuming.

Radha was doing all the household chores and cooking for both her brothers and herself. Sometimes Ashok used to go and catch some fish from the pond and Radha used to get excited about cooking the fish. Radha was not exceptional but she was a reasonably good-looking girl, and she had a rare talent – she could sing very well. She sang devotional songs and modern songs.

They had a distant female cousin who was in the music business. She used to take Radha to villages for marriages and Puja festivals, and Radha started making some money from it. So Radha knew all the rich people near and far. Someone also offered her the chance to sing for a record. As her elder brother, Ashok was in two mind as to whether to allow her to follow her talent or to restrict her – but he came up with a solution. Even though the sister would be there at the functions, he wanted Aditya to accompany her. Aditya was not at all keen but Ashok insisted, so he had no choice but to go.

During one of the functions, a wife of one of the rich men liked Radha and her singing. She had a young son and was looking for a suitable girl. She told Radha's cousin that she would happy to have Radha as her daughter-in-law. The cousin said she would inform Ashok, who would make the final decision. Not now, said Ashok.

Money was very tight. Somehow Ashok managed all the expenditure for food, clothing, education and all the festivals. Radha used to cook on very tight expenses and their food was basic. Rice was free because it came from the land, while fish was also free because they had two well-stocked ponds and Ashok would catch fish at the weekend.

The land around the house was very fertile. They had a few plants producing aubergines, cauliflower, marrows and chillies. Oil was expensive, but they used mustard oil for cooking and coconut oil for their hair. They would boil the juice from the huge number of date and plum trees to make black sugar.

Ashok was saving money to buy a cycle, but he couldn't accumulate enough. So he had to walk to the village market, which was about three miles away. In the rainy season it was impossible. In the summer, mid-day was very hot. They would go out only if it was absolutely essential.

Ashok was also worried about saving because he knew he would need a fair sum for Radha's marriage. Although his mother had kept some gold in a jewellery box, and his uncle Dhruva had promised some because he had no children, Radha's marriage was his responsibility as her brother.

Ashok told some of the friends he was looking for evening and weekend work because he needed money for his forthcoming exam. One of Ashok's friends told him his aunt was looking for somebody for part-time cooking; they were pretty well off and would be quite happy to pay him. Ashok had no idea about cooking, but his friend suggested he go and see Mrs Choudhury and see what she said.

After thinking about it for a few days, one Saturday Ashok turned up at the address his friend gave him – a big, mansion type of house – and met the motherly Mrs Choudhury. He said: "Ma'am, I am studying for my matriculation, so Monday to Friday I am very busy. But over the weekend, if you want, I will be happy to help you in the kitchen."

Mrs Choudhury said: "I am not looking for a full-time cook, as I already have one. But seeing that you are an honest young man who wants to earn some money, I have plenty of work and you can come and work on Saturday and Sunday."

Then she asked Ashok: "Have you cooked before?"

"Never in my life," said Ashok.

Mrs Choudhury said: "Fair enough. We will teach you."

Mrs Choudhury was generous enough to promise him a good salary for two days' work. So, Ashok thought, at least financially he would be much better off. He also thought Mrs Choudhury was a nice, motherly lady. From the following weekend Ashok started going to the Choudhurys' house and soon realised that actually she didn't need any more help. She just wanted to help Ashok out.

Another thing happened. The Choudhurys had a big temple and Mrs Choudhury used to worship for a long time and Ashok, being Brahmin, was told to come to the temple and help Mrs Choudhury. Ashok, being a likable and polite chap, was liked by everybody in the household. Mrs Choudhury started looking after Ashok as her own son.

Ashok's house had two good-sized bedrooms and a kitchen. The toilet was outside, surrounded by various trees. Radha lived in the inside room, which had a door. The other, doorless room was where Ashok and Aditya would sleep, eat and do everything. They had two beds in the corners of the room. Ashok's was very neat but Aditya's was untidy. Ashok's side was full of books, pens and pencils and writing paper.

With the help of Mrs Choudhury, Ashok managed to buy a second-hand cycle. So, instead of getting up at three o'clock on Saturdays, he got up at five to go to Mrs Choudhury's house. At that time, everybody in the family was still in bed. Ashok started bringing some books for his exam so that, whenever he got a chance, he could read some papers. Also, his lunch and dinner had become free. He also learned some cooking, but the Choudhurys were strict vegetarians – not even eating onions or garlic.

Ashok would sit and have a little bit of breakfast. There were two earthen ovens. He would take them outside to start a fire in them and, when they were well lit, would bring them inside. By six o'clock the main cook arrived, and he would tell Ashok to wash and cut the vegetables and grind all the spices in a hand-held grinder. By that time, the Choudhury family would have their breakfast and Mrs Choudhury would come to the kitchen and tell them what to cook. She would have some *Betel* nuts and go for a shower.

After an hour or so Ashok would be summoned to the Puja Ghar, so he cleaned his face, hands and feet with tube well water and went to the temple. Mrs Choudhury sat on a stool and started the puja, while Ashok sat on the floor lighting all the candles and lamps.

After the family had their lunch, Ashok had free time between two and four o' clock. Mrs Choudhury, sitting on the veranda, would read the *Ramayana or Mahabharata*, while Ashok revised his maths. Although the weekend job took its toll on Ashok, because he was always worried about Radha and what Aditya was up to, he was very well treated. He got good money and free meals and the work was not too tedious.

Radha had a few friends among the girls from the village and, because she sang at several places, many people came to know that Radha Banerjee was a promising singer. One day Ashok was in the Choudhurys' house when one of Mrs Choudhury's friends, from a land-owning family, came for lunch. Seeing Ashok, she recognised that he was in her son's class.

She asked Ashok: "Radha, the girl who was singing the other day, is she your sister? She is not only pretty, she sings very well."

She didn't say any more but, before leaving, she told Mrs Choudhury: "I wouldn't mind my son marrying Radha, because they are of our caste."

Mrs Choudhury said: "Do you realise they have no parents and they have no money?"

The lady said: "That doesn't bother us."

The following week, Mrs Choudhury told Ashok about the proposal. The boy's name was Apurva Mukherjee and his family owned quite a bit of land. Ashok knew the boy and thought it was not a bad idea, but he asked Mrs Choudhury: "I have only one sister, I want her to get married well. I will take your advice. What do you think?"

Mrs Choudhury said: "Your sister will be very lucky. They are good people."

On the Sunday evening, Ashok cycled as fast as he could to reach home. It was nine o'clock and dark when he arrived.

Radha was waiting outside the house with a small kerosene lamp. Aditya was sitting on the veranda eating. Radha said: "You took a long time to come. We have been waiting for you. Go and have a dip in the pond so that we can eat together."

But Ashok was too excited. He said to Radha: "Come inside the bedroom."

Radha came with the lamp. Ashok told her to sit on the bed and Aditya sat down with her. Ashok said: "I am going to ask you a very serious question. You can take your time, but I need an answer."

Radha said: "What is it?"

Ashok said: "How do you like the boy Apurva Mukherjee from the next village?" Before Radha could say anything, Aditya said: "I know him. He beat me up in a football match for nothing."

Ashok shouted at Aditya: "Shut up! I didn't ask you."

Radha became hesitant and shy and said: "I have seen him once in a marriage party. He seems to be OK but why do you want to know that?"

Ashok said: "Apurva's mother has seen you and liked you. They want you to marry Apurva."

Radha hesitated again, kept her head down and said: "I will do whatever you suggest."

Ashok said: "In that case, I will go to Apurva's house and talk to his parents about fixing up a date."

In India, most marriages take place in the winter. The *Durga Puja* and *Diwali* are the two biggest festivals and they happen before winter sets in and when the rainy season is over. The harvest comes out during the autumn and winter months. There is plenty of food and vegetables and you get a variety of sweets – maybe that was the reason. Hindu marriages take place between November and March; after that it becomes too hot. The marriage functions place more responsibility on the bride's side. They have to make most of the arrangements and feed a large number of people.

But the elders of the family hold all the discussions and take all the decisions about the marriage. Ashok felt he needed to discuss the matter with his uncle Dhruva and his aunt Bina.

One evening he turned up at their house and Dhruva shouted to his wife: "Come out, Ashok has come."

His aunt came out. Ashok touched their feet, she gave him a glass of juice and they all sat on the veranda. Ashok said: "I came to see how you people are doing. But I also have to take some advice and guidance from you about a serious matter. We have got a very good marriage proposal from the next village. The boy used to be in my school, he's called Apurva. They are Mukherjee Brahmin."

Dhruva said: "I know the family very well and Apurva is a nice lad. It's a good match. When do you plan for *pati-patra* and the marriage?"

Ashok said: "For that I need some help from you."

Dhruva said: "Don't worry, Radha is like our daughter. Your aunt will look after all the marriage festivals." The aunt nodded her head with acceptance. "As for me, you just tell me what you want me to do and I will do it."

Ashok said: "I was planning for the marriage in March, so, we have four months. In January I have got my final matriculation exam, so I want to finish it first."

Dhruva said: "That sounds good, but you haven't told us what you want us to do." The aunt went and got some sweets and food for Ashok, then said: "Don't hesitate, be open and tell us: how can we help?"

Ashok said: "Working in the Choudhurys' house, I have saved some money but it is not enough. I need at least a couple of thousand rupees because I want to give Radha a good marriage."

Dhruva said: "Two thousand rupees? That's a big ask. I can give you some money and I can borrow some from a friend, but it will be tight. Why don't you give a slightly lower-key marriage? Your parents are dead, so people will understand you cannot spend a lot of money. Also, at your age I don't want you to have a big loan. On top of that, you have to look after Aditya too."

Ashok kept quiet for some time, then said: "I have thought about a plan, provided you don't mind. I was thinking of selling some land from our side and taking the money for the marriage."

Dhruva got up and started walking around. He looked disturbed by the idea. He sat down again and, putting his hand to his head, said: "No. No, you can't sell our parental land to an outsider. Then what happens to your house?"

Ashok said: "I was not going to sell the house. I was going to sell the land around the pond and that would fetch a couple of thousand rupees."

Dhruva became angry and started shaking. He said: "That land borders my land. So what happens to that?"

The aunt calmed them down and said: "Listen, both of you. Radha is like our daughter and your parents are no more, so, we will come up with some idea. Give us a couple of days to think over it."

Ashok said: "We cannot let this proposal go out of our hand. The boy's family has some demands."

Dhruva said: "Your aunt is right. Let's think it through with a cool head. Give us a couple of days and I am sure we will have some solutions. In the meantime, you tell the Mukherjees we are happy to proceed with the marriage."

Ashok was not very happy but, hoping for the best, he slowly walked home. He saw somebody swimming in the pond in the dark and knew who that would be. He shouted: "Aditya, come out. Let's go home."

By now Aditya was growing up and going to the main school in the village, which was in the teacher's house. The brothers walked home, where Radha was standing outside. She said: "I have been waiting for you guys. Come on, I have cooked some hilsa fish."

The three of them sat on the floor to eat fish and rice. Ashok said to Aditya and Radha: "I must tell you, I have spoken to our uncle and aunt. We are going to finalise Radha's marriage with Apurva."

Aditya said: "What about her singing? Would they allow her to sing?"

Ashok said: "That's for later. The plan is to have the marriage in March next year. We will need some money and uncle Dhruva has promised he will give me some money, but I told him I will take it as a loan and will give it back. I have also spoken to Mrs Choudhury. She will be kind enough, if needed, to loan me some money."

Radha said: "Are you sure you want to take a loan for my marriage?"

Ashok said: "Of course, I am 100 per cent sure. Me and Aditya want to give you a good send-off."

Aditya said: "What happens if you don't get the loan?"

Ashok said: "I have decided that in that case we will sell part of land next to the pond."

Radha said: "No. No, don't sell our land. In that case I am not going to get married if you have to go through hardship."

Ashok said: "Don't worry, Radha. Once I do my matriculation, I will get a good job."

Three or four days passed. One evening, Ashok was reading a book when he heard his uncle shouting: "Ashok, are you at home?"

Ashok and Radha both came out. Both touched his feet, Radha got a chair for her uncle and gave him a cold glass of water.

Dhruva said to Radha: "I have some private discussion with Ashok. So leave us alone for few minutes." Then he whispered to Ashok: "After discussing with your aunt, we have come up with a solution.

"We have no children and your aunt has a large amount of gold which she doesn't use or wear. Radha is like a daughter to her. It is her decision that she will sell part of the gold and that will give the two thousand rupees you need. We don't need to sell our ancestral land."

Ashok said: "No, no. You can't do that. I can't take that money."

But Dhruva said: "Your aunt is very strong minded. Once she decides, you can't change her mind. When you get a good job, you can pay me back. Also, part of the land you have got is lying idle. If you allow me, I could ask Abdul to farm the land and we could share the profit."

Ashok gave a sigh of relief. He said: "I have to ask again, do you want to do that, uncle?"

"No ifs, no buts, 100 per cent. So next week, you fix up a day for *pati-patra*."

CHAPTER 5

One Saturday afternoon Ashok, his aunt, uncle and a *pandit* went to the Mukherjees' house. They sat in a circle on the veranda. The *pandit* took a piece of paper and started writing down who was getting married to whom, their dates of birth and their ancestors' names. So, it was decided and finalised that in the first week of March the marriage would take place in Ashok's ancestors' house.

Ashok was happy to fulfil the demand the Mukherjees had. He had only one request on behalf of Radha, that if she got an invitation to sing to all of India on the radio she would be allowed to accept it. The Mukherjee family were happy to agree.

On the way back, Ashok was relieved but very tired. In six weeks' time he had his matriculation exams. He was working very hard to get a grade A so that he could get a decent job. He had some money and gave it to aunt Dhruva to buy some saris and dresses for Radha. The aunt said the market would open in the next village the following month, so she would go and buy there. This year's harvest had been very good, so people had plenty to eat and drink.

Ashok's matriculation exam was modelled by the British Board of Education. It had two languages, English and one local tongue. The other subjects were Mathematics, History, Geography and Economics. This was run by the board of Calcutta University from two centres, one in Calcutta and one in Dhaka. It had three grades, first division, second division and third division – and fail.

Third division was a basic pass at 40 per cent. Second division was 60%. And first division was 80% - you could get star or letter marks after that. Ashok was expecting at least a first division. Over the years he had worked very hard and he was very mature for his age. He had looked after his responsibilities very well. Now he had to get his sister married and to look after his younger brother, who was more interested in playing football and kabaddi than studying.

Ashok had to go to the main village school to take his exam. He got a new *dhoti* and Punjabi and slippers from the village shop. He got a bottle of ink, a pen and blotting paper. Now his admit card also arrived. He kept everything organised on the table and he was very tense – Aditya and Radha were staying out of his way.

Before the exam, Radha did some puja, gave some flowers to Ashok to carry in his pocket and tied a thread on his wrist. Ashok was having difficulty sleeping because of the tension. Before the day of the exam he went to school and took the blessings of his teachers.

In those days matriculation was a big event in the village; only one or two boys would sit the exam. Ashok touched the feet of his head teacher, a nice, polite gentleman who said to Ashok: "I am confident you will do very well. Keep your cool, read the questions well and write as neatly as you can."

Ashok's exam centre was in Malanda, about a three-mile walk away. The exams were starting at 11, so he planned to leave home at eight o'clock. There were seven consecutive days of exams, and on each the ritual was the same. Ashok woke up at dawn, did a bit of revision, put some oil on his head and had a quick dip in the pond. Aditya was sleeping but Radha gave him a bowl of milk with two home-made chapatis with some sugar. After he had changed, Radha put a *tilak* on his forehead and wished him luck before Ashok set off.

Ashok felt the exams were tough, but hoped he had done enough to get a good grade. After the exams were finished, he went and saw his headmaster to tell him how they had gone. The headmaster was confident that Ashok would get first class.

Now the exams were over, the biggest challenge for Ashok was to organise a grand marriage for Radha. First of all, he had to make a list of all the people they would invite, and to print the invitations. He took Aditya with him to choose the card and decided the invitation should be given in the name of his uncle Dhruva because he was the eldest in the family. The printer told him what to write. Then he took Aditya to organise the supply of all the food, vegetables and flowers for the marriage.

His uncle organised somebody to make a *pandal* for the marriage and to organise four cooks to come and cook for at least the whole week, including the marriage feast. Ashok was not worried about fish; he was sure someone would be able to catch enough with a net from their own pond.

In the middle of this, he got a call from Aditya's head teacher to come and see him regarding Aditya's behaviour in school. The head said Aditya had become a bit disruptive and his discipline had been called into question a few times. The head teacher felt he lacked motivation and needed stricter guardianship.

Ashok was very annoyed but reassured the head teacher he would have a strong word with Aditya. Ashok sat down with Aditya and told him what the head teacher said, and he added: "Unless you get educated, no way we can get out of this trap. If you don't educate yourself, your only option will be to do farming with our uncle."

Two weeks before Radha's marriage, Ashok's result was due to come out. Because there were only a handful of students taking matriculation, the names of those who had passed were hung on a board outside Dhaka College or Calcutta University. Ashok decided to go to Dhaka on a Monday morning. Radha asked him to buy a few things for her from Sukhobaspur. From home, he had to walk a couple of miles to get to the Ganges. From there you had to take a steamer to go to Dhaka, and from there it was a walk of a mile to the College.

Ashok used to go to Dhaka only if it was required. But he knew the route and he had ten rupees in his pocket. Early that morning he set off for Dhaka College. Dhaka is a beautiful city. It was a centre of culture in British India on the bank of the Ganges, with green spaces and big Building was designed by Mughal and English.

Dhaka College was a tall building with many students. He asked one of the *peons*: "Where are the results hung?" The *peon* said: "You are lucky, we have just hung them this morning."

Ashok became a bit apprehensive and walked slowly towards a big, black board. There was an A4 piece of paper pasted on it saying the names and grades of successful candidates for this year's matriculation. Ashok had difficulty focusing and looking for his name but soon he was elated when he saw Ashok Chandra Bandyopadhyay: first class with distinction in Mathematics. He couldn't believe his eyes. He literally jumped with joy.

Once the adrenaline calmed down, he realised just how hungry he was. He went to a local restaurant and had some fish curry and rice, then immediately started walking towards home because he wanted to give the good news to Radha and Aditya himself. In the evening he reached home with his printed certificate and the grade. The main certificate was posted home six weeks later.

He informed all the people in the village, his teachers and his uncle Dhruva. His uncle was delighted, congratulated him and gave him 10 rupees to celebrate. He asked Ashok what his plan was. Ashok said: "First we will get Radha married and then I will look for a job."

His uncle said: "With your percentage of marks and distinction you will get a job in no time." But Ashok had to think about where to apply because, after Radha was married, he had the responsibility of Aditya.

By the following week Ashok became a local celebrity. No one in that village or any of the ones nearby had passed matriculation. He was congratulated by many people. Radha's marriage activities were going on steadily, but Ashok had other worries that most of the good jobs were in Calcutta. What happened if he got a job in Calcutta; where would Aditya go?

Because of the marriage, Ashok was meeting his uncle every evening to discuss matters, so he raised the issue: "What if I get a job in Calcutta?"

Dhruva said: "First of all, get the job – then I can give you a solution. Listen, we have a very big house. We are only two people who live with servants and maidservants. If you have to go to Calcutta, Adi can move in with us. He won't need to change school and friends. And he will be very well looked after by his *Chachi*. I am sure Adi will love that, rather than being dragged to Calcutta."

Ashok said: "I am very reassured. That sounds very good thinking indeed."

Ashok told Aditya lots of people were coming for the marriage and they had better clean and paint the whole house. Both went to the town, got some paint and painted the whole house themselves. They got some people to put up a big *pandal* with a platform in the middle for decoration for the marriage, then built another *pandal* in the back of house for guests to eat, and a temporary kitchen in the middle.

Their aunt had organised all her clothes and gold ornaments. Most of the people were given money in advance and the local sweet store was supplying all the sweets.

The question arose, who would give Radha away? Ashok said to Dhruva: "In absence of our father, I think it would be right if you give away Radha." Dhruva was delighted to play the role.

Ashok organised everything meticulously. The musicians started playing their *shehnai* in the morning and all the guests began to turn up wearing fantastic *saris* and *dhotis*. They sat on the chairs around the platform and at about five o'clock Apurva and his party turned up with the *pandit*.

Aditya and his friends brought Radha out with her head covered. The musicians played and the *pandit* chanted in front of the fire. Apurva and Radha circled around the fire and took the marriage vows. All the guests had a large amount of food and sweets, and all said what a nice marriage it was.

The following morning, Apurva and Radha sat in a *palki* and left Sukhobaspur for his village. Radha was crying inconsolably, though she looked stunning in all her new clothes and jewellery. Both her brothers were standing numb, as if the world had come to a sudden end.

At Radha's house, the in-laws had thrown a few parties for the marriage because they were very well off. Ashok, Aditya and their aunt and uncle, with a few village people, came to Radha's house. After a day everybody went back to their own homes. Ashok and Aditya both felt that without Radha the house was empty.

CHAPTER 6

Ashok started looking at the national newspaper's job section and applying for positions. Most of the managerial jobs in the early years of the 20th century were in Calcutta because all the big companies were owned by the British Government. For managerial posts, they wanted people who had matriculated and could read and write English.

So Ashok went to the town hall to look at the English paper and got a passport picture of himself to attach with the applications, which all started: *"Respected Sir, I the undersigned humbly apply for the post…"*

In the meantime, he had a long chat with Aditya and told him the only way he could do well was if Ashok got a job – but that job might be far away. He also told him of the discussion he'd had with their uncle and aunt and that they were more than happy to put up with him.

Ashok also said Radha's marriage had gone over budget. He had incurred a lot of loans from people and was now planning to pay them back. The other option was for Adi to go with Ashok wherever he got a job. Aditya didn't like either of the options; he said: "Why can't I stay alone in the house?" Ashok reminded him he was still a minor and couldn't live alone. Aditya didn't answer and left the room in a teenage grump.

After six weeks Ashok got two interviews in Calcutta. However, one job was for the railways and the other was teaching in a high school. Another possibility was working for a British company in North Bengal. This was interesting because it was for a multi-national company. The salary grades were very good, and a bungalow and a servant came with the job. The job was with a company called Skipton, based in Ambari near Darjeeling. It was a financial job, as a manager.

Going for all the interviews was not financially possible, but the Ambari job interested Ashok because it was in the foothills of the Himalayas.

It was a tea-estate employing about 500 people that had its own small school and hospital, with a full-time doctor and a compounder. The interview would be at Skipton's head office in Dalhousie Square, which was bang in the middle of Calcutta.

Ashok informed them he was keen on the job, so he got a date and time and the address of the office in the post for his interview. He thought if he got this job he would be able to pay back his loan very quickly. Ashok bought a new suitcase and a fine new *dhoti* and Punjabi – he had new palm shoes already.

When Ashok told Mrs Choudhury he was going for an interview, she insisted he wear a long black jacket. She told him she would ensure her tailor made it for him. He went to the tailor and sorted the jacket out.

Ashok would need to stay for two days. The interview was at 12 o'clock and he wouldn't be able to get there in time unless he travelled overnight. However, Ashok didn't know anyone in Calcutta well enough to stay with. Mrs Choudhury solved that problem too.

She said: "My brother Bishwanath has a studio and top floor flat in Bowbazar. The business is on the first and second floor, but they live on the top floor. I will give you a letter to give to Bishwanath. he is my younger brother. I am sure he can sort out your food and accommodation. If he can't do it himself, he knows a lot of people. He will sort you out."

Going from Sukhobaspur to Calcutta was not simple. First you had to walk nearly three miles a place called Goalanda, where you took a steamer, which crossed the old Ganges three or four times a day. From there you walked about half a mile to Dhaka's main station, in an area called the *Cantonment*. There was a train in the night at 10 o'clock called the East Bengal Express from Dhaka to Calcutta. This overnight train arrived at six o'clock in the morning at a rail station called Sealdah, which was in the centre of Calcutta.

One day, as the interview grew near, Ashok got up early and left with his suitcase, which held his new clothes and a letter from Mrs

Choudhury, and about 100 rupees in the pocket. Aditya came with him to the steamer and they talked as they walked before Ashok bought a ticket for the steamer and got a seat in the corner for the crossing, which took about an hour.

Because this steamer was going to the city of Dhaka, it was full of farmers with their produce and chicken and goats. It was very noisy, untidy and overcrowded. The British had brought a few discarded steamers from Southampton to India to work as ferries.

Ashok gave Adi five rupees and said: "Behave yourself until I come back. I will be home within a week."

"Don't worry," Adi said, "I am sure you will get the job."

The steamer, with its big siren, slowly started turning towards the North. Ashok had a bit of lunch and all sorts of things went through his mind. Luckily it was not raining and after an hour or so he arrived on the Dhaka side. Foot passengers were allowed off first and Ashok disembarked with his suitcase and asked a few people where the main Dhaka rail station was. He was not in a hurry because the train did not go until 10 o'clock at night.

He arrived outside the rail station, a big, beautiful building with arches. It looked majestic. He went and bought his ticket and he was told he could book a sleeper if he paid five rupees extra. Ashok agreed. He told the ticket checker he had eight hours to spend and the gentleman said: "You could leave your bag here and walk around Dhaka – you will like it."

Dhaka was the second biggest city in Bengal and had many rivers. The city had been ruled by Hindus, Buddhists, Mughals and now the British. Ashok walked around the city. He was not hungry, but he decided to eat something because he might not get anything on the train. He had some *poori* and vegetables with some sweets and, in due time, he came back to board his train. He had an open return ticket that he'd bought for three rupees – a lot of money in those days.

He slowly walked back to Dhaka Central. There was a big, long train with a steam engine blowing out huge plumes of smoke. Emblazoned across the front was British East India Railways. There were five compartments. There was first class, which was only for English people and Government officials. There was no second class, only third class. But if you bought a ticket with a bunker, you could sit by the window and in the night could sleep on the top berth. Ashok had one of these tickets.

But the last compartment was the biggest one. All the fresh vegetables and other products of East Bengal used to go to the West of Bengal and far away in India. Transporting goods was big business that was usually conducted by boat from one part of Bengal to the other.

There was a ticket checker in a black coat with a black board in hand who had all the passengers' names, compartments and seat numbers. A few people were harassing this guard but Ashok waited patiently. When it was his turn, he was told his seat was number 16 in Compartment B. He also asked the checker what time he expected the train to arrive at Sealdah. The gentleman said: "If all goes well, it should arrive at 5am."

Ashok got into the compartment and sat down. There was a gentleman opposite who introduced himself as Mr Kalam and they started chatting. While they were talking, the guard gave a whistle and waved his green flag, the steam engine driver gave a big whistle through his hooter, pulling a white rope, and the train gently but steadily moved off from the station.

As the train slowly picked up speed, Ashok could see beautiful scenery through the window. The river flowing, the boats sailing on it and all the lovely birds and flowers. Kalam offered him some sweets, saying they were made by his wife. Ashok didn't want to upset him, so he took one sweet from him. They started talking about the British Raj, unemployment and the conflict between Hindus and Muslims.

Ashok agreed the religious friction was getting very worrying and hoped things would stay as peaceful as they had been over the years. Ashok found the discussion was enjoyable but after some time he gave an excuse and said: "I need a bit of sleep and I am going to the top bunker to lie down."

This was an express train that used to stop at only two stations. One of them was Ranaghat. Ashok said to Kalam *Bhai*: "Can you wake me up when it comes to Ranaghat?" Kalam said: "No problem."

Ashok put his bag under his head as his pillow and tried to read a paper. At about midnight, with a big jolt, the train stopped. Ashok woke up and came down from his bunker. Kalam *Bhai* said: "This is your Ranaghat. The train will stop here for 20 minutes as they refuel the coal, so we could go out and stretch our legs and have tea."

They came out and walked in the station with two pots of tea in mud cups. Kalam said: "If you are going to stay in Calcutta for three days, where are you going to stay?" By now, both of them had become friendly and Kalam said: "If you have difficulty, you can come with me. My son lives in Park Circus. He is single. He will come to pick me up. If you have any problem, you can come and stay with us for a couple of nights."

Ashok said: "That's very kind of you. But I have got a letter for a gentleman who is the brother of Mrs Choudhury, from my village. I am expecting him to come to collect me and I will stay in Bowbazar in his flat."

Ashok came to know Mr Kalam very well. He was a big farmer in East Bengal and a member of the Congress Party. Kalam wrote down his address on a piece of paper, gave it to Ashok and said: "I am very impressed talking to you. You are my son's age. If you need any help or have any problem in Calcutta, you come and stay with me."

The train moved off again. Ashok went to sleep; he had so much to think about and he was extremely tired. When he woke there was a lot of noise and people running around and the train was stopping. He came down and got everything organised. He had arrived at last in Calcutta.

Kalam said: "Best of luck for the interview, but Calcutta is a big city. Look after your money and possessions carefully."

Ashok said: "I am grateful for your blessing."

They both departed to either side of Sealdah station. Ashok came out and the checker asked him for the ticket. Ashok gave him the ticket and said: "It's a return ticket." The checker punched it and gave it back to Ashok.

Ashok was standing in front of the passengers' waiting area, where he was supposed to be picked up by Bishwanath. Ashok had never seen him, so he was looking at everybody's face in a place full of people. Suddenly a very well-dressed middle-aged man walked up to Ashok and said: "*Namaste*. I am Bishwanath. I am sure you are Ashok. I have heard so much about you from my *didi*."

Ashok said: "I hope you have heard something nice."

Bishwanath laughed and said: "Come on. Give me your bag."

"No, it's fine. Thanks," said Ashok, "I will carry it."

They discussed the journey and Bish said: "My business is in Bowbazar. It's about a mile from here. First we could go to a restaurant and eat, or we could go to our place so you can have a shower and then go out."

Ashok said: "It's entirely up to you."

Bish said: "In that case let's go home. It's five minutes' walk – let's walk then. I understand your interview is on Monday at Dalhousie Square. So, plenty of time -I will take you there. Almost every day, I get a request from someone coming from our village to Calcutta and wanting to stay with me. I politely decline but when *didi* asked me, I took one second to say yes."

Bowbazar Street was a long street. It crossed Harrison Street and at the junction was Sealdah station. Although these roads were very wide, there was a tram line in the middle and all sorts of shops on each side – the vendors even had shops on the footpath. There were a lot of people to-ing and fro-ing and there was the hooting of the bus. It all made it a very vibrant and lively city.

After five minutes' walk they arrived at the junction of Bowbazar Street and Armar Street and Bish pointed to the house in front and said: "This is our palace." It was a Victorian house. On the ground floor was a the Sarkar Brothers jewellery store, while on the first floor was Bish's photographic studio and on the third were two rooms and a small kitchen.

Bishwanath was a very jovial man, with a nice sense of humour. He employed two people and had got a lot of contacts at the colleges of Calcutta University. These contacts had all been made through people from the village. Every year he got a contract for the universities' and colleges' identity cards and all the photographic requirements, which he delivered. He also got a lot of marriage photographic contract – overall, he made a good living

He had a few Roliflex cameras, a studio for taking pictures and a dark room for developing them. He appointed a distant nephew, Manik, as his assistant to carry all the luggage for him, deliver all the pictures and collect the money for his uncle. Manik stayed in one of the rooms next to the kitchen and cooked for himself. He seemed to know Calcutta inside out.

Bishwanath had also bought a house in an area of South Calcutta called Ballygunge, a 20-minute bus or tram journey from his studio. The studio was open every day except Sunday, although it was also closed on days when they attended big functions. He had had to invest in decorating the studio, and bought some chairs and sofas for taking portraits of people and their families.

When Bishwanath's work ran late and it was difficult to get a bus or tram home, he slept in the top floor room, which had two beds. One of the beds he kept for guests – some of them were nice, some less so. Some made too many demands of Bishwanath, not understanding he had a business to run. But having Manik there was very helpful.

Staying on the third floor room had two disadvantages. The toilet was on the ground floor, and so was the tube well. That was why Manik kept two buckets full of water all the time in the kitchen.

Bishwanath was married. He lived with his wife and one son in Ballygunge. He got up early every morning and, after a shower, he did puja in Sanskrit for an hour. At 10 o'clock he would have a breakfast-cum-lunch. Usually he liked boiled rice with butter and two boiled eggs.

He was very fussy about his clothes because in his business he had to present well, so he wore a very high-quality *dhoti* and Punjabi. Then he would take his umbrella and walk to the tram depot, which was not far away. He always got a seat and within 20 minutes he had arrived at his studio.

By now Manik had opened the studio and given the whole place a good clean. There were always one or two customers during the day needing passport pictures, or ladies requiring their marriage proposal pictures. After one o'clock Bishwanath would start his main business, going to the PR department of the colleges and the university, or some sporting club, for his next assignments.

Through his contacts, he had recently got entry to Fort William, the barracks for English civilians and soldiers. Bish could speak a bit of English, so he started picking up a lot of business from there.

Bish told Ashok: "I will take you to your room. You must be very tired. Have a lie down and I will come back by five o'clock. Although Manik can cook well, I will take you to a dining place this evening."

Ashok entered the room and said: "Oh, that's a nice room with a nice bed."

Bish asked him: "Do you need a blanket?"

"No, that will be fine," said Ashok. Bish gave him a newspaper and Manik brought a glass of water. Ashok changed and lay down but by the time he looked at the headlines in the paper he fell into a deep sleep.

In the meantime, Bishwanath had a few places to go to for appointments. He was running late, and a couple were waiting in the studio for their portrait. He asked Manik to organise the portrait, but Bish knew people liked him to take the pictures. Although he was running late, he took the pictures of the couple and told Manik to look after Ashok if he needed anything. Bish came out and jumped on a tram that was heading to Esplanade. This was the city centre of Calcutta, built by the English on the banks of the Ganges.

Ashok had a good sleep. After all, he had been travelling for 18 hours or more. He came down and saw Manik was sleeping on a chair. He thought he would not disturb Manik but Manik woke up and said: "Did you sleep well? Do you want to have a shower?" Ashok thought that was a very good idea. Manik gave him a towel and showed him the ground floor tube well.

The water supply in Calcutta was refined from the Ganges and rainwater. So the water was thicker and a bit cooler than the village water Ashok was used to. Ashok had a good shower and changed.

At about 5.30pm Bish came back huffing and puffing with a big smile on his face. He said: "I am sorry, I got delayed – but I was late to start with."

Ashok asked him how his day was and Bish gave a big smile and said: "I got a new contract for taking photographs of all the employees of the Port Commission."

Calcutta was the biggest port in Asia. Cargo ships would go from Calcutta all over the world, particularly to England. It employed a large number of people, but most of the jobs were menial jobs and most of the employees were Muslims. The commission's headquarters were in Khidirpur, where Bish would be going every day for some time to take all the pictures. It was a good contract and he was a happy man.

He said to Ashok: "Get ready, we are going for dinner. It will be a bit early, but I have to go back home."

Ashok combed his hair and said: "Let's go."

Bish said to Manik: "Do you want to come?"

Manik said: "No, I have already cooked at home."

Bish said: "Close the shop and I will see you tomorrow." They came out into Bowbazar Street and Ashok was surprised to see that Bish was very popular. Everybody was bowing and saying *"Namaste"* to him.

On the corner of the road was a huge church. Bish said this was the Anglican church. The British had built it and the inside was excellent, with pictures and statues. Ashok had seen a few churches before, but nothing like this.

Bish was pleasant and he liked talking. He asked Ashok: "Did Manik look after you well? I am very worried about that lad. I have given him a job because he is the son of a poor widow, but he is getting a bit smart and he has become too friendly with the jewellery shop owner's daughter. The jewellers are not the same caste as Manik and Mr Sarkar told me that, although he likes Manik, he won't let his daughter marry him.

"I have told Manik a few times, he keeps laughing and telling me, 'Don't worry. Things have changed, inter-caste marriage is not an issue'. Although he is a nice, likable lad, I have told him that if he doesn't listen to me he will have to look for another job. You see he didn't come with us? The only reason is that he will go down and talk to the girl downstairs."

Bish added: "I will take you to Putiram Kitchen. It's an authentic kitchen on Dharmatala Road and it's about a two-mile walk. If you are happy, we could easily walk. It's a nice day and you could see the bustling city of Calcutta and when we finish dinner I will drop you to Bowbazar before going to my house in Ballygunge. But I have to take the tram by 10 o'clock because after 10 it stops."

Ashok said that was plenty of time and Bish started asking how the rainfall had been back in the village and how the harvesting was going. The general discussion went on until suddenly they arrived in front of a restaurant with a big board on the top saying Putiram Kitchen.

Both entered the restaurant. It was well decorated, with enough tables and chairs for many people to sit and dine. One elderly gentleman came forward to Bishwanath and welcomed him: *"Namaste."* Bishwanath said to Ashok: "This is Putiram *Babu,* who owns the restaurant and he comes from the next village to ours back home." Then he said to Putiram *Babu:* "This is the brightest boy from our whole area. He has got distinction and first class in matriculation. He is here for an interview, so might come here tomorrow for dinner."

Putiram *Babu* said: "It's an honour. I haven't seen any matriculated person in my life. I will give you a nice hilsa fish curry and rice."

"That sounds good," said Ashok, who was very hungry. He tucked in quickly but before that both he and Bish did the Hindu ritual to give some food for God and the hungry. Putiram *Babu* sent *rasgullas* and said that they were on him – there was no need to pay for that. Ashok said goodbye to Putiram *Babu* and said he hoped to see him the next day.

Ashok and Bish started walking towards Bowbazar and suddenly Bish said: "Do you want some *paan*? They sell it on the corner of the road."

Ashok said: "Thank you but I don't eat *paan*, nor do I smoke. If you want to, go ahead and have it." So, Bishwanath had a large *paan* and had difficulty in talking with it stuffed in his mouth while explaining about things in Calcutta.

Bish said: "Tomorrow is a holiday so the studio is closed. I normally don't come to the studio but because you are here, I will turn up in the afternoon and will ask Manik to make lunch for you."

As they talked they neared the studio. Bish said goodbye to Ashok and jumped on a tram and shouted: "See you tomorrow."

Manik was standing outside the studio and asked Ashok if he'd had a nice meal. They went to the top floor and Manik gave him a glass of water and asked if he needed anything else.

Ashok said: "Can I have a book to read, please?" Manik came back with a book by Tagore that Ashok had read many times, but he thanked Manik and went to his room. He lay on the bed and, before he could think, he fell asleep.

Early in the morning Ashok woke up to lot of noise and commotion. He didn't realise that Bowbazar market, one of the biggest markets in Calcutta, was on the corner of the road. At dawn all the farmers brought produce from nearby villages to sell.

Manik came and gave him a cup of tea. Ashok said: "Thank you. I normally don't take tea but as you have kindly made it, I will have it."

Ashok was very impressed with Manik. He said to him: "What's your future plan? Manik said, "I don't like studying. In the village school I was failing every year and I was becoming a burden to my mother, who is a widow. We knew Bishwanath *Babu* through a contact. He kindly gave me the job and also, I like the city. I don't like a quiet and dull village life."

Ashok said: "Is it true what I hear? That you are having an affair with the daughter of the jeweller."

Manik said: "How do you know that?"

Ashok said: "When I came, I saw the girl standing behind you."

Manik said: "We are Brahmins and the girl's family are low caste. But if the girl would like to marry me and she is the only daughter of the Sarkars, I will get involved with the business and my life will be set."

Ashok said: "I don't believe in the caste system. But if you want, I can talk to Bish."

Manik said: "No. Bishwanath *Babu* is a very orthodox Brahmin. He will not accept inter-caste marriage."

"Then what are you going to do?"

"That's what I am thinking about all the time. Bishwanath *Babu* has given us a living for not only me but also for my mother. It won't be easy. But in the end I have to choose one. It will be hard, but I will marry the girl and run their business."

Ashok said: "What about the Sarkars?"

"They don't want to upset anybody. Their business is very stable, and they won't mind their daughter marrying me because she is the only daughter and if she says something, the parents will agree."

Manik then made two omelettes, two toasts and a cup of tea. Ashok did a small puja before lunch and thanked Manik, telling him he needn't have cooked so much.

After lunch, Ashok stood on the balcony. Even though it was a holiday, the street was still full of people running around with eggs, milk and vegetables. He was absorbed in the beauty and the life of Calcutta.

Bish came in the afternoon, took him out to show him more of the city; the multiple markets, shop after shop, the bank of the Ganges, many multi-storey houses and a few hotels and after that the big empty space called the *Maidan*. It was a green area with trees.

There were a lot of football clubs scattered around it. The famous ones were East Bengal, Mohun Bagan – still in existence, and India's oldest current team - Mohammedan Sporting and a few others. The sport had been introduced to the country by the British Army and it had become hugely popular among the locals.

Its spread was attributed to a teenager from Calcutta, Nagendra Prasad Sarbadhikari. A bright, energetic student of Hare School, with deep brown eyes, gangly limbs and a bouncing walking style, his passion for what he had seen the Army play convinced his British teachers to train him and others in the game.

Sarbadhikari helped start many clubs. Calcutta FC was the first to be established in 1872, with others following quickly. This made the city the de facto football capital of India and earning Sarbadhikari the title "the father of Indian football".

1888 saw the introduction of the Durand Cup (the third oldest competition in the world after the FA Cup and the Scottish Cup). Royal Scots Fusiliers were the inaugural winners, beating Highland Light Infantry 2–1 in the Final. In 1893 the IFA Shield was founded as the fourth oldest trophy in the world. In those days football was the favourite sport among the people of India – not cricket.

At the end of the *Maidan* was the British army barracks called Fort William. About 40,000 soldiers and civilians were stationed there. Behind that was the large Victorian memorial hall, a huge white marble building made by Prince Albert. You could go inside but could not touch anything.

And then the beautiful river Ganges, which flows down from the Himalayas and through the cities of Bengal. There were few bridges but lots of boats. As the sun set, there was a rainbow in the sky.

Ashok was stunned by the sheer beauty and peace of the place. Suddenly he got a tap on his back and Bishwanath said: "Where are you lost, my friend? Let's go and eat something."

CHAPTER 7

On the Sunday, Bishwanath took Ashok to meet a friend from the village whose name was Satya. Bishwanath and Satya had been friends at school before Satya moved to Calcutta to start a business. After struggling for two or three years he had opened a tailor's shop near Manicktala – a poorer suburb in Northern Calutta - specialising in making trousers. Because trousers were a new thing in India and not a lot of people made them, his business started doing well and, with his earnings reasonably good, he bought a house near Manicktala.

Bish and Ashok took a tram from Sealdah to Manicktala. The tram made lots of noise, cracking and clunking, with a continuous bell ringing in the background, fruitlessly trying to tell walking commuters to move from the line ahead. It took nearly an hour and after walking for a few minutes, they arrived outside Satya's shop.

Although the shop was closed because it was the weekend, Satya was waiting outside. The shop was not a big one. There was an iron gate and a big board on top of the shop saying Matri Tailor. Satya embraced Ashok and they talked for a few minutes about the news from their village, where a small-scale riot was going on between Hindus and Muslims.

Bish introduced Satya to Ashok, who soon realised that Satya was heavily involved in politics. He was a regular member of the Quit India movement. He was also an active member of a party called Hindu Mahasabha.

Satya said the religious problem was getting more and more acute in Bengal and there were rumours the state would be divided in two. As he was very involved in the resistance to the idea, he said there were tensions in the village around temples and mosques.

Ashok said: "Although my village is predominantly Hindu, there is also a sizeable Muslim population. My uncle has a farm and 80 per cent of his employees are Muslims. But we get on very well with them and we have a close family relationship with them - so we have no issues in our place."

They decided to have some food and talk more about their village. Satya had a friend called Mohammed Altaf who ran a restaurant, where they went to have something to eat. They found that all three of them, although non-vegetarian, didn't eat beef. They had a good discussion on national and international matters sports, and a big fight over who would pay the bill. In the end Satya insisted that this was his home town now, so he should pay. Satya said goodbye to Ashok and added: "I am sure you will get the job. When you come back, you must come to my place."

Bish said: "On the way we could go to Firangi Temple."

"What is that?" asked Ashok.

Bish said: "The story goes that a young bride was put on the cremation fire of her old husband. But an Englishman called Anthony saved the girl and decided to marry her and, because normal temples wouldn't allow him to marry, he decided to open his own temple of Kali, became a Hindu and married this beautiful young girl. Since then people think this Kali temple is very lucky and very popular."

The temple was on the way home, so they went there. There was evening *Aarti* in progress so they sat there for a few minutes, gave *Aarti* and came out. Still talking, they slowly reached Bowbazar Street.

Bish said: "I will say goodbye to you now. Your interview is at 11 o'clock at Skipton House, which is next to the Writer's Building in Dalhousie Square. I go there almost every day, so I know the place. I will come early at seven o'clock tomorrow morning. You rest tonight and do some homework for tomorrow.

"I will take you with me, so you don't need to worry. Ask Manik to iron your shirt and *dhoti* and make sure your shoes are polished. The English are very particular about that.

"By the way, have you got a good pen? If not, I will give you my pen tomorrow. I have a good Pelican pen. Your *Boudi* will do some puja for you and I will bring some flowers."

Bishwanath disappeared. It was still early evening, so Ashok started practising some questions in his mind and answering them over and over. Manik took his *dhoti* and shirt and bought them back ironed. Ashok pondered for a long time and walked around the roof of the house, wondering what would happen if he did or didn't get the job. He lay in bed looking at the roof, tossing and turning, and didn't sleep very well.

After he woke up, by seven o'clock he had had a shower and he was ready. He had two pieces of toast that Manik made. At about eight o'clock he heard the thick, loud voice of Bish giving instructions to Manik. Ashok thought Bish looked smarter and better dressed than him.

Bish said: "Ashok, do some puja, which is important, and get ready. We have to go."

Ashok combed his black hair and tried to look like a real *Babu*. Bish said: "Let me have a look at your interview papers. OK, it's at Skipton House, one of the biggest buildings in Dalhousie Square. In that case we'll go to the tram depot and take a direct tram there."

They got the tram and sat together. Bish bought two tickets but Ashok was very serious, and he couldn't concentrate. Bish kept telling him that with his qualification and personality, the English would like him. "Be smart," he said, "You will be fine in the interview."

They arrived in Dalhousie Square, the biggest in the city of Calcutta. It was the hub of Government machinery. It was surrounded by big red-brick houses and there were small islands full of multi-coloured flowers. There were some sitting stools. The whole place was spick and span because the cleaners cleaned the square every morning with water from the Ganges.

They walked for 50 yards or so and came to a big, smart, yellow building, five storeys high with golden letters saying Skipton House. Skipton was a large British conglomerate that did business in tea, confectionery, soaps and other essential goods. It was 100 per cent British owned.

It was an hour before the interview but Bish suggested that Ashok went in and took a seat. Ashok entered the building, which was cool because they kept the temperature down by spraying cold water on to jute curtains. There was a gentleman sitting at the reception desk and Ashok showed him his interview papers and asked him where to go.

The gentleman said: "OK, you are supposed to be on the fifth floor, so you could take a lift or the stairs. When you get there you will see an office of the PA to the Director. He will show you where to go."

Ashok had applied for the job of Manager in a large tea estate in Ambari, not far from the district town of Siliguri. The nearest big town was Darjeeling. It was in the northernmost part of Bengal, in the foothills of Himalayas.

Bish said: "I have to go. Best of luck to you. Go to the fifth floor. I will come back and see you here at three o'clock outside the gate."

Ashok got in the lift and the lift operator asked him: "Where do you want to go?"

He said: "I am going to the office of Mr Thomas Neil, the Director."

"Have you got an appointment?"

"Yes, I have got an interview."

They went to the fifth floor, which had three offices. One was Mr Neil's, one was his secretary's and next to them was the PA's office. There was also what looked like a big boardroom next to that. Ashok knocked on the door of the PA and said: "I am here for the interview for the Manager's job."

The PA looked at the paper and said: "Yes, that's correct. But you are a bit early. Mr Neil hasn't come yet but he is a very punctual man. He will like that you are in before time. Don't worry, your interview will start at exactly 11am."

He showed Ashok into the next room, invited him to sit on a chair and asked if he would like tea or water. Ashok declined.

He sat down, and time passed slowly. Ashok started getting slightly restless. He was given a job description and a booklet about Skipton. There were five candidates and Ashok seemed to be the first. He tried to visualise the map of West Bengal and think where Ambari was.

From the booklet he found out that Ambari was in the foothills of the Himalayas. It rained a lot and it was very cold and hilly, but it was also a healthy place. Because water didn't stay on the slopes, the tea plant grew better there. Tea plants are not very tall, reaching about waist height. They produce a large amount of green and yellow leaves and they grow themselves. You don't need to nurture them, just plant them.

When the leaves were ripe they were picked, mostly by tribal ladies. The north of Bengal had a large number of tribal people from Nepal and Sikkim. Once the leaves were picked they were dried, roasted, cut into pieces and packaged for supply all over the world.

Skipton was one of the largest tea producers and suppliers in the world. They were looking for a chap for this job who had a basic qualification of matriculation, who was good at man management and who would be good at accountancy too. The monthly salary was pretty good and it came with a two-bedroom house with a kitchen and garden. The company would provide a house servant too.

The estate also had medical facilities with its own doctor and a small dispensary with two compounders. But travelling there was difficult. There was a train from Calcutta, the Jalpaiguri Express. From Jalpaiguri you could take a bus, cycle or a taxi, if available, to reach Ambari. Walking from the rail station was hard; it was several miles, all uphill.

Exactly at 11 o'clock, Mr Neil's PA came out and said: "Mr Banerjee. Mr Neil will see you now."

He took Ashok to the boardroom. There was a horseshoe-shaped table, around which five people were sitting. The chairman of the panel introduced himself; this was Thomas Neil. He was in his mid-fifties with grey hair and a big, bulky stature. With him were the company accountant, another director, the PA and a company HR person. The chairman started asking questions and said they were very impressed with Ashok's CV and grades, but he hadn't any experience of work. How would he compensate for that?

Ashok explained that you have to start at some stage. Unless he was given a chance, how could he prove himself? He felt Mr Neil was nodding his head to his answers. The interview lasted an hour, which passed very quickly. Ashok was told he could go home and be sent the result by post – or he could wait until 3pm, when he would be told the outcome.

Ashok decided to wait. He went out for a while and came back again. At two o'clock he saw the last candidate come out.

It was a long wait. Most probably, they couldn't make up their mind and it was a long discussion. At about three o'clock, Mr Neil came out of the office and said: "Mr Malone, can you come to the boardroom?"

Ashok thought his chance had gone but the PA smiled and said: "Mr Banerjee, would you mind waiting? Mr Neil wants to have a word with you."

Mr Malone went in and Ashok sat and wondered why on earth they wanted him to wait. The other three candidates wished him luck and left.

After Mr Malone came out, they called Ashok into the room. Mr Neil said: "Mr Banerjee, we are very impressed with your interview. You are the only guy who hasn't got any experience of managing anything, but I feel you have got a bright future in this company if you consider taking the Assistant Manager's post.

"Mr Malone was acting as assistant manager and we have promoted him to the managerial job. If you are happy to accept, you can work with him because he knows the job and the place well - he will be able to teach you from the scratch."

Ashok knew he needed a job badly and without hesitation he said: "I am very grateful for the offer and I understand that I need to learn a lot. I will be happy to accept the job. But I will need a couple of months to join because I have a young brother I need to sort out. That will take some time and also, if you permit me, I want to do my graduation in Economics and Accounting. I will need some help from the company."

Mr Neil stood up, shook hands with him and said: "That's not a problem. Welcome to the company. My PA will let you know the details and the salary and the perks of the job." Three other directors shook hands with him too and wished him good luck.

Ashok came out with a big smile on his face and saw Mr Malone waiting there. He came over and said: "My name is John Malone. You can call me John. I have been in Ambari for a year or more and I will be able to tell you everything about the job. I look forward to welcoming you there.

"I am from London. At the end of the year I plan to visit my mother for a month. I expect you to pick up the job quickly because, with travelling in a boat to England and staying there, it will be altogether two months." Ashok said: "Don't worry."

Ashok came out of the Skipton building and saw Bish was sitting on a stool opposite. He ran over and asked: "What's the news?"

Ashok said: "I got a job. Not the manager's job, but the assistant manager's job."

Bish gave him a hug and said: "What does it matter? It's important that you got a job. Let's go and celebrate. You must be hungry, let's go to the K C Das sweet store."

They walked across the road to the oldest sweet store in Calcutta and Bish ordered a large amount of sweets and snacks. Ashok wanted to pay but Bish said: "Today it's on me."

He asked: "When do you plan to join?"

Ashok said: "I have asked them to give me two months. They will give me a salary with a house, a cook and a servant. Also, they will pay for the transfer of my luggage."

Bish said: "That is a good thing about having a job in British firm. They look after you well."

Ashok said: "When I go for the job, I might go via your place."

Bish said: "That will be excellent, but this time you will stay in our house. My wife will be delighted to look after you."

Ashok said: "At the present time, my biggest worry is my younger brother Aditya. He is very attached to me and also, he is neglecting his studies. If I get a good school in Ambari, I might take him with me."

Bish said: "That's a very tribal area. Getting a good secondary school for him will be difficult. Also, taking him from deep in the east of Bengal to the north will be a cultural shock for him. Could he stay with your sister Radha? I understand Radha is very close to Aditya."

Ashok said: "Radha's in-laws are well off but I don't know them or Apurva very well. I thought about it and I am going to have a chat with Radha and Apurva when I go back.

"But the best option is on the table already. My uncle and aunt have no children. They like Adi very much. They already said not to disrupt Adi's education. He will be better off staying with them. I am torn in my mind as to what is best to do. What do you think?"

Bish said: "Look, you need a job. Without earning, you won't be able to maintain yourself and Adi. To me, the only choice is to keep Adi with your uncle. And you could visit him every couple of months. He doesn't need to change anything."

Ashok was due to return home the following day. After the interview he felt very tired and he needed to wake up early. He said to Bish: "I need to buy some sweets in three packets. One for Adi, one for my uncle and one for your wife."

The following morning, Ashok woke up early and packed all his bags. Manik gave him a cup of tea. He gave Manik a big hug and said: "Thanks very much for looking after me. In a couple of months, I will come back to join the job and go via here."

Ashok already knew how to get to Sealdah station. The train that came from Dhaka arrived at Sealdah and went back to Dhaka after a few hours, once the engine was checked for water and coal and the crew was changed.

Ashok had a return ticket already. He arrived a bit early and got a seat next to the window – he wanted to see the scenic beauty of rural Bengal. As the train was about to start, a round man came huffing and puffing, got on the train and asked Ashok: "Is this the train to Dhaka?"

Ashok said it was and the man sat opposite to him and introduced himself: "My name is Tapan Sikdar. I am from Faridpur and we run a business of *paan* leaves. We supply everywhere, so I come to Calcutta more or less every week and stay in a bed and breakfast. It's a fixed place near the university and the owner is also from Faridpur."

He asked Ashok the purpose of his visit and Ashok told him. He asked Tapan: "How are things in your part of the world?"

Tapan said: "It is not good. Faridpur was a very peaceful and bustling town but in the last couple of years there has been a huge amount of religious tension. Only last month quite a few people were killed, both Hindus and Muslims – a total waste of life.

"We've run our business for a few generations and we employ a large number of people because it is a labour-intensive business. But the workers are 50-50 Hindus and Muslims and the tension has built up all the time, particularly during *Puja and Ramadan*.

"Recently there was a big killing in our village. The whole thing started with two young boys fighting during a game of marbles and that got out of hand."

Tapan offered Ashok a *Biri* but Ashok declined. Tapan lit his *Biri* and said: "I will speak in a low voice because there are a lot of Muslims in the compartment. The problem is that many believe whatever the rumour goes.

"A lot of Muslim people work for me. They are very good people, decent and peaceful. But there are always a few trouble makers. So, during this marble game there was an argument among a few boys of eight or nine about cheating. They started fighting and they beat this Muslim boy black and blue.

"So in the evening some of the Muslim youths turned up in the village with knives, swords and lathis. Some of the young Hindus didn't like it and a full-scale riot started. A lot of houses were burned. The brunt of the damage fell on poor Hindus and Muslims. These people are already on the periphery of society and hardly get enough to eat – now they have an added worry about religion.

"I was in Calcutta at the time. When I went back I couldn't believe my eyes. Many houses and livestock were burned and so many people had lost their lives.

"My brother and I, with a few of our Muslim workers, called the local *Imam* and called all the young Hindu and Muslim boys to an open-air meeting. Everyone agreed it was a terrible thing to happen in our village, which is like a big family. Everybody agreed not to provoke any more hostility. Now the village is quiet and peaceful. But I am really, really worried about the future."

Ashok said: "Yes, in my part of the world the tension is becoming quite palpable nowadays. I have a very little holding but my uncle has a lot of land and recently many of his land workers have converted to Islam. They are all good, hard-working, decent people and they all love my uncle. He is the breadwinner for them and they love him, but every month there is a mini-riot around Dhaka and that news comes back to our villages.

"Recently in Dhaka there was a riot because during a Ramadan procession somebody deliberately threw a pig's head. But there is talk of dividing Bengal. I hope it never happens. Tapan *Babu*, we have to accept we are a minority in our own land from a religious point of view."

The train was passing through the beautiful green land of Bengal as it went from west to east. The train stopped at Ranaghat Junction and Tapan said: "Come on Ashok, I will buy you a cup of tea. I was listening to a young lady singing some devotional songs on the radio. They introduced her and said she grew up in your village."

Ashok's eyes lit up and he said: "That's my young sister, Radha Chatterjee. Now she is married. When I go home, I plan to see her."

Tapan said: "She really sings very well."

Ashok said: "Thank you. She was trying to be on the radio, so you made my day."

The train set off again through the rain. It was a few hours before they reached the Dhaka *Cantonment*. Tapan took a piece of paper, wrote his name and address and gave them to Ashok, saying: "It was such a pleasure to meet a bright young man like you. I would like you to come and stay with us if you can make some time." Ashok said he would try his best.

He looked through the window. There were acres and acres of paddy fields, interspersed with grounds full of boys playing football bare chested. In other places they were playing kabaddi and when the train crossed under bridges Ashok could see the fishermen hard at work.

On the train a hawker was selling some mangoes. Ashok decided to buy five for Adi and put them in the bag. There was another hour to go. Ashok was getting very impatient and couldn't sit still. He started loitering in the corridor of the train.

Eventually, the train stopped at the majestic Dhaka station. Tapan embraced Ashok and said: "Once again, it will be a pleasure if you can come to our place. I've said it before, but I promise you will be well looked after." Ashok agreed and promised to visit.

Ashok left the train with his bags and ran towards the jetty because he knew the ferry crossed every two hours. The steamer was hooting to show it was about to set off in a few minutes. The steamers were supposed to take about 40 people with some fruit and vegetables, but in reality, more than 100 would get on board, with lots of groceries and sometimes even cattle. The steamers were made in Belfast and were sturdy and relatively safe.

Ashok, huffing and puffing, got a ticket and jumped on to the steamer. There was no place to sit and it was very congested. He wondered whether these ships were safe, but he was not worried – he was a very good swimmer. Even in high school he could cross the Ganges.

The steamer slowly started. The river was rough and turbulent, but the steamer made a U-turn and sailed gently across the river. Everybody wanted to reach home before it got dark because there were no street lights and you had to go down the muddy roads from your memory. Again, this was not an issue because Ashok had passed along these roads many times.

When he reached the other side it started raining but Ashok had an umbrella and he started walking home as quickly as he could.

He knew the village like the back of his hand. In those days there was no lock on your front door, so when he arrived home in the dark he couldn't see anything. But he knew where the lamp was. He put his bag in the bedroom and shouted Adi's name a few times. There was no response, so he took the lamp and went out to look for him.

He had some idea where Adi might be, so he took the umbrella and lamp and walked to uncle Dhruva's house. His uncle was mending a fence and Ashok said: "Have you seen Adi?"

His uncle said: "Yes, he is having a meal in our kitchen. Your aunt is feeding him."

Ashok gave a sigh of relief and said: "Thank God!"

Dhruva asked: "How did the interview go?"

Ashok said: "It was good, and I got the job."

"I knew it. Very well done."

Ashok said: "I will take Adi home now. I will come back tomorrow and talk to you about a few other things in detail."

Ashok went in and saw Adi sitting on the floor eating home-made cake with both hands and his aunt sitting on a chair. Ashok said: "Adi, I was looking for you everywhere."

Adi said: "When did you come? I didn't know you were coming now."

His aunt said: "Ashok, have some cake."

"No aunty, I will go home. I am very tired. I will come back to talk to you and uncle tomorrow."

His aunt said: "OK, have dinner with us tomorrow."

Ashok and Adi went home. Ashok said: "Let me have a shower in the pond and then I will cook something, and we will talk."

He cooked some boiled rice and boiled potatoes with some butter and they sat down to eat.

Ashok said: "I have got the job. It's a very good job in an English firm with a good salary."

Adi asked: "Is it in Calcutta?"

"Not really. It's in north Bengal on the foothills of the Himalayas, a place called Ambari, which is not far from Darjeeling.

Adi made a face. "I am not going there."

"You are only 14. You cannot stay alone."

"What do you mean by staying alone? What am I supposed to do then?"

Ashok said: "You have to understand. We don't have a lot of money or a lot of business. I need a job to support both of us. There is no job around here, so I have to go wherever the job comes along. For a short time, we might have to adjust but as soon as I get settled you will come and stay with me."

Adi said: "What if you don't settle? What do I do?"

Ashok said: "Go to sleep now. Next week you and I will go to Radha's house and we will discuss it further."

Adi was happy with that. Ashok had two months in hand to sort out all the issues.

The next Monday, Ashok and Adi got ready. They got some presents for Radha and her in-laws and started walking along the bank of the river towards Radha's in-laws'. Ashok was not very clear about how to find Radha's house but he knew it vaguely. He said: "If need be, we will ask the villagers for directions."

Radha's in-laws were relatively well off. They had a lot of farming land and a nice house with a big garden. Radha lived with her husband Apurva and his parents, brother and sister. Before midday Ashok and Adi were near Radha's house when they met Apurva. He was surprised, but happy to see them. He said: "Welcome to our village and come to our house."

One thing Ashok observed was that Radha's family were very conservative. Radha had become a fully-fledged housewife. She was delighted to see both her brothers and asked them to come inside her bedroom. She was wearing a costly sari with lots of ornaments and she had a veil covering her forehead. Then Radha's in-laws came, insisted that they stay and asked Radha to cook some delicacies for her brothers.

Adi gave two *saris* to Radha, one for her and one for her mother-in-law. Ashok gave her a bag full of mangoes from his village. They stayed but Ashok found it difficult to talk to Radha alone. Apurva took them the following day for a boat ride to see the local stunning scenry on both sides of the river and there was a boat man who sang a few songs. That evening they had a big meal and in the morning Ashok said quietly to Radha that he needed to talk to her.

After breakfast he said to her: "I need some advice and a favour. I have got a job in north Bengal." Radha was delighted to hear that.

He added: "But I cannot take Adi with me to start with. I am going to ask you something. If you are not sure, tell me – I won't mind."

Radha said: "Do ask."

Ashok said: "If I asked you to keep Adi with your family for a few months, what do you think?"

Radha paused and said: "It would be a delight to keep Adi, but you have to understand this is not my house, this is my in-laws' house. From what I know of them, between you and me my mother-in-law may not like the idea."

Ashok said: "That's fine. I thought it might be difficult for you, so I understand fully. Don't speak to anybody about this matter, it's as if this discussion never happened."

He added: "I was very proud that you are singing very well, and you sang on All India Radio."

Radha said: "Thank you *dada*, but I might give up singing."

Ashok was shocked and said: "Why on earth would you want to do that?"

"Both my in-laws don't like me going out singing. They think I should concentrate on giving them a grandchild and forget about singing now."

Ashok felt like crying. He said: "Your in-laws promised me that they would let you sing – otherwise, I wouldn't have fixed this marriage."

Radha said: "You can't do very much about it. It's not your fault. It's my fate and if it keeps everybody happy then I have no choice."

After lunch, Ashok and Adi said goodbye. Radha was upset to see them go but Ashok was very angry with the in-laws for not allowing Radha to pursue her career in singing.

While coming home, Ashok realised that Adi wouldn't be able to stay with Radha because Radha's in-laws were very inward-looking, conservative people and there seemed to be some friction because Radha was not allowed to sing. She was getting well paid, but her in-laws were not interested in the money because they were well-off.

Ashok was more upset because he felt that Radha had a bright future in music. On balance, Ashok was glad he'd asked Radha about Adi, but it was not to be. Ashok realised that, maybe for a few months, Adi would have to stay with their uncle and aunt while he tried to organise a permanent solution. It would be best to sit down with them and Adi and have an open discussion.

That night, Ashok called Adi to his bedroom. He said: "Adi, I have never been away from you since you were born, but you have to understand that the time has come. I have to do some earning and, as I told you, it's a very good, well-paid British job. It will be very difficult to arrive at the job with you and, as I said, our uncle and aunt are so keen to keep you and you don't need to change the village, your school and your friends.

"Give me a few months. I will make sure that I take you with me because otherwise I will miss you too much. I have already asked about schools in Ambari. As soon as I go there, I will take it further as I will have a bungalow to stay in."

Adi kept quiet. He said: "If that is the choice, that's fine. I know aunt Bina likes me very much."

Ashok said: "Why don't we go to their house tomorrow evening to finalise the arrangements? In the meantime, there is a market on Thursday in the village centre – you tell me things you need and we'll go together and buy it."

"OK," said Adi. "I will make a list."

Ashok was very relieved that Adi was happy to give it a try. He knew in his mind that Adi would be safe and secure with their uncle and aunt.

The next day, Ashok decided to meet his head teacher. He went to his house and started shouting: "Sir, are you at home?"

The head teacher came out and said: "Ashok, come in."

They both sat under the tree outside the house. Ashok said: "Sir, I have got a job in north Bengal, so I will be leaving in a few weeks' time. Adi will stay with our uncle Dhruva uncle and aunt Bina. You know them."

The head teacher said: "I have known Dhruva for a long time. He is a nice man. I am sure he will look after Adi very well."

Ashok said: "I want to talk to you about Adi."

The head teacher said: "The problem is, Adi is not keen on education. A vocational training could be a better idea."

Ashok said: "I will look into it Sir, but please look after Adi as long as he is under your guidance."

The head teacher said: "You had better stay and have some lunch with me."

Ashok politely declined and said: "Sir, I have to go and buy a few things. But I promise, when I come back from Calcutta I will definitely come and have dinner with you."

Time passed very quickly and soon there were only a few days left before Ashok was departing for north Bengal. Ashok bought a big suitcase and new clothes; a *dhoti* and Punjabi and all the essentials. It cost him nearly 50 rupees.

He was getting more anxious. In 26 years he had never left the village. Also, since his parents died, he had looked after Adi as both a son and brother. Lately he had heard that after school Adi was mixing with some rough young men and hanging around the market town.

Another big worry was the religious tension. All his life, Hindus and Muslims had lived very peacefully in the village like one big family. Almost all of uncle Dhruva's employees were Muslims and his right-hand man, Abdul, called Bina "aunty". But recently the tension among the communities had become palpable, particularly during religious festivals. This could erupt into violence any time.

About a week before departing, Ashok sent a telegram from his village post office to the Calcutta head office saying he would arrive in Ambari by the North Bengal Express on a certain date. He got a letter from the Company saying somebody would be there to receive him.

On the day of his journey, Ashok was very upset. He packed all his bags and uncle Dhruva came with a few flowers that aunt Bina gave from her puja. He touched the flowers to his head and put them in his pocket. He gave some money to Adi and said to keep it in case of emergency.

The three of them came out of the house before Ashok had a good cry in front of his parent's photographs – then he locked the door and gave the key to his uncle. Dhruva said: "Adi and I are coming to the banks of the Ganges. Don't you worry about us, and don't worry about Adi at all – as you know, aunt Bina will look after him as her own."

It was a one-mile walk. Ashok could hardly say anything because he was so upset. They neared the boat, Adi carrying his bag. Ashok got a ticket, hugged uncle Dhruva and touched his feet. He said to Adi: "I will be back soon." He could hardly say any more because he had a feeling of choking.

Ashok got on the boat. The steamer had started hooting that it would leave in a few minutes. The sun was going down in a clear sky with a gentle breeze. Ashok stood at the end of the boat.

Slowly the steamer started. Ashok, with all the weight of the world on his shoulders, looked towards the bank and kept waving to Adi and Dhruva. Slowly, they got smaller and smaller as the steamer moved deep into the Ganges. There was a singer on the boat. He was singing a lovely folk song about departing, as if he knew what was going through Ashok's mind.

Dhruva said to Adi: "Let's go to your home. I have asked Mansoor to come to pack up your books and luggage."

Adi said: "I can pack myself."

Dhruva said: "That's fine. We could all give a hand and you will be sleeping in the next bedroom to ours. So take all your luggage there. And this weekend there is an open market in the village. You and I will go together and buy anything you need or fancy for your room. I think you need a big mirror for your hairstyle, which we will buy."

Adi gently nodded. After an hour they arrived home. Dhruva opened the door and said: "Adi, come on. Start packing. I will go and find Mansoor. If you leave anything behind, we could always come back tomorrow and fetch it."

From Adi's house to Dhruva's house was not far. Adi packed up all his luggage and Dhruva told Mansoor not to take any utensils or furniture. It was getting late.

Dhruva came out with both of them and put a padlock on the front door, even though in those days it was rarely required. Mansoor had a cart and he put all the luggage on and started pulling it.

Adi arrived at his uncle's house. His aunt Bina was standing outside. She gave a big hug to Adi to welcome him and gave him a cheese sweet. They went inside and Mansoor put all the luggage in the room, which already had a bed, table and chair. Bina put statues of two deities, Radha and Krishna, on the table, then brought a small *Bhagavad Gita* and touched that book to Adi's head before putting it next to the deities.

CHAPTER 8

The steamer arrived on time in Dhaka and Ashok boarded the East Bengal Express. He had a seat and a sleeping bunk. He had travelled on this train before, so he knew what to expect. This time he had decided to stay a couple of days with Bishwanath in Calcutta before taking another train to Jalpaiguri. He had a big suitcase and a holdall full of useful belongings.

The train was relatively empty, so he put the bag on a seat and took his holdall to his bunk. Ashok was not in a mood to talk to anybody, although there was one family travelling to Calcutta. His mind was full of worry about leaving Adi and he couldn't work out whether the decision he had taken was the right one – would it have been better to stay in the village for a few more years working with uncle Dhruva? He could have tried for a job in a couple of years' time, when Adi would be much more mature.

Thinking all these things, Ashok fell asleep. Suddenly, for the second time in succession, he was awoken with a jolt by the shouts of people searching for *coolies*. Ashok realised he had arrived at Sealdah, the main station in Calcutta. He got off the train with all his luggage and saw a smiling man standing far away and waving at him. He soon realised it was Bish.

Bish came over and gave him a big hug. "I knew the train was two hours late today, but I came with Manik," said Bish, "but he had to go to see his mother. We have to carry the luggage ourselves."

One *coolie* was shouting behind but Bish said: "No, we are all right." While they walked, Bish asked Ashok what his plans were. Ashok said: "Thursday and Friday I will be at your mercy. Saturday, I plan to travel up North. Sunday I'll rest and Monday I start the job."

Bish said: "Simple as that. At least Ambari is a hilly station with good weather, good food and lots of fresh air. Did you inform them when you are arriving?" Ashok said: "Yes, I have telegraphed them."

They went to Bish's upstairs flat to store all of Ashok's luggage, then Bish said: "You freshen up, then we will go to our house. You will be staying here because my house is very small. This flat will be more comfortable for you."

Ashok said: "That doesn't bother me." Ashok and Bish went to their house in Ballygunge, where Bish's wife made a feast. There were five different types of fish, and Ashok had a very good meal.

The following morning, Bish and his wife came and took him to the Kali temple at Dakshineswar. Bish said to Ashok: "This is our most important God, do a puja for the blessing of the goddess Kali."

Ashok did and he felt very humble and sober. He liked Bish's wife. She told him that Bish thought of Ashok as his own brother, and he was very touched by that. On the Saturday, Bish and Ashok, with Manik carrying all the luggage, went to the rail station to put Ashok on the North Bengal Express.

This was a beautiful train. It had more horse-power because it had to climb uphill on its way up North. First class was particularly pleasant because Darjeeling was the most scenic town in the foothills of Himalayas. Many English people wanted to have a break in the summer and they travelled to Darjeeling. Lots of hotels and tourist entertainments were situated there.

Ashok got his seat in the right place in the train and told Bish: "I will not forget your hospitality."

Bish said: "I want you to be back whenever you can."

Ashok also said to Manik: "If you decide to marry the jeweller's daughter, give me a shout and I will be there."

The train moved off. Ashok started reading a book, but the beautiful scenery was breath-taking. After a few hours the train arrived at Jalpaiguri. He got off the train with his luggage and looked around for anybody from the company. Suddenly he saw Mr Malone was standing in the corner of the station. Ashok was not expecting that.

Malone came and shook hands and said: "Welcome to Skipton Company and welcome to Ambari." He asked him about the journey, then took him outside to a company jeep. They put the luggage in the back and Malone drove off.

The beauty of the place was breath-taking and Ashok could see why so many English people from Calcutta came here, particularly to Kangchenjunga – the second highest Himalayan peak after Everest.

Ashok was very excited about the new place and job, but also tense and nervous. Malone was driving, Ashok sat next to him and the driver sat in the back. The roads were very hilly and bumpy.

After about half an hour's drive they arrived outside a beautiful bungalow on a small hilltop and Malone said: "Ashok, this is your place. The driver will take the luggage."

Then a teenager came up and said: "Sir, I am Ramu. I will be staying with you as your servant." Ashok invited Malone in but Malone said he had already seen the bungalow and it was beautiful.

"I will go now," he added. "Tomorrow is Sunday. Rest. Our office is only a quarter of a mile from here. You could walk but, with Monday being your first day, I will send my driver to pick you up."

Malone left. Ashok and Ramu took the luggage inside the bungalow. It had two bedrooms, a good-sized living room and an attached toilet and bathroom. At the back there was the kitchen-cum-dining room. The master bedroom had a double bed with one table and chair and a large *almirah* with a mirror attached to it.

The sitting room was not very well organised. It had lots of books, newspapers and old journals scattered around on the big table and a chair. The bathroom and the toilet were basic. The kitchen had two earthen ovens and a small portable oven that was lit with coal outside the house and brought in.

There was a tube well outside the house. It had a tin shade on top and was covered at the sides. So you could have a shower under the tube well and go back through the kitchen into the house without anybody seeing you.

Ramu put all the luggage in the bedroom and said: *"Babu,* the whole house has been painted because you were coming. I will cook something."

Ashok said: "You understand that I am vegetarian but eat fish?"

Ramu said he had already bought some rice, lentils and some potatoes, so he could make some *Khichri* with boiled potatoes and *Ghee.* Ashok said that was fine.

Ramu said: *"Babu,* if you give me some money I will go to Ambari and buy some fresh vegetables." Ashok gave him five rupees and had a good shower under the tube well. The water seemed to be different here, very fresh but also very cold, because it was not far from the Himalayas.

He enjoyed the hot *Khichri* Ramu cooked but he was very tired. He went to bed, telling Ramu he would unpack everything tomorrow, and within a minute was asleep.

Ashok woke up with the morning sun through the window on his face. Ramu brought him tea, then Ashok wandered around the bungalow. The beauty of the surroundings was different from the scenery around the Ganges and his village. Both were beautiful and charming, but they were totally different.

Ramu said: *"Babu,* today is Sunday. We have a small market today but Thursday is market day in Ambari."

Ashok said: "Let me get ready. I will come with you to see the market."

Ramu was the guide; he knew the town well. He was a half-caste boy. In the north of Bengal there were lots of tribes and Bengalis and Assamese mixed people. Through the centuries the Nepalese, Sikkimese and Bhutanese had come down from the foothills of the Himalayas to the plains, with Indo-Chinese features. The story goes that Gautam Buddha came through the same way from Nepal to Bengal and then to Bihar.

The village people were very friendly. As they walked around, Ashok was stopped by many people as they realised he was the new man in the job. They all said "*Namaste*" and wished him good luck. He enjoyed his walk. At the end of the road the sky seemed to be joining the earth.

After half a mile, there were a few people with their produce sitting around in a circle. There were fruits, vegetables, chicken, bags and slippers. All were shouting for customers and calling their prices. Ramu started introducing Ashok to everybody, saying he was the new boss.

Ashok bought some vegetables and fruit. While coming back, Ramu asked what he wanted him to cook. Ashok said: "Cook whatever you fancy but tomorrow I have to wake up a bit early. As this is my first day at the job I need to be there before eight o'clock."

Ramu said: "Don't worry. I will take you there because I know that the Englishman has got an office there." Ashok realised that Malone was a sort of celebrity around the town – and the only white man.

After dinner Ashok went to bed thinking about Adi and decided to write a letter. He wrote: "My dear Adi…" but couldn't decide what to write next. His thoughts were clouded by his emotions. It was the first time he had left his brother alone. He couldn't write any more before he fell asleep.

In the morning, Ramu said: "*Babu*, I have ironed your shirt and *dhoti* and polished your shoes also."

Ashok had a shower and came back and did puja with *Gayatri Mantra*, which he did all his life. He got changed and ready and took the fountain pen that Radha had given him on his birthday. He said to Ramu: "Mr Malone said he will send the car, but let's walk."

On his first day at work, Ashok was there at half-past seven sharp. He told Ramu to go back but before he went, Ramu said he would turn up at half-past five to take him home.

Ashok entered the office. It was a large, long office with rows of chairs and tables on both sides and at the end of the hall, there were two offices. On the door of one was written Manager: Mr Malone. On the next one, in gold letters on a board, was written Assistant Manager: Mr Ashok Banerjee.

There was a man sitting on a stool outside his office. He stood up and said: "*Namaste*, Banerjee *Sahib*." After a few minutes Mr Malone arrived. He was a tall, lanky man, originally from London, with a soft Cockney accent. He had been working at the East India Company in London and, after he lost his wife to cancer, he decided to join the Skipton International Company and took a posting to India.

In those days, only the brightest British people would get jobs in India because it was the chance to move away from damp, cold England. Malone had come to India and he enjoyed every minute of it.

He shook hands with Ashok and said: "Welcome officially to Skipton Industries." Then he took him to the middle of office, where everybody stood up, and he said: "This is Mr Ashok Banerjee. He will be deputy to me and he will be in charge of all of you." He invited Ashok to his office and told the *peon* to bring two cups of tea.

They sat, and Mr Malone said: "Let me introduce you to some of the facts and figures of this estate. Soon, you will know everything. This job was too much for one manager, which is why you will be sharing most of the job. But I will supervise and guide you.

"I know it's your first job but any time you have any worries, don't hesitate to ask me. I may not have all the answers but, having done managerial work for some time, I will be able to tell you what to do and what not to do.

"Please call me John. I live in the big bungalow behind the office on top of the hill. A few years ago, my wife died in London due to cancer, so I decided to venture out here and I love it here. But I go back to England once a year because I have an elderly mother.

"I love this country and I love the job. We employ about 1,000 people on the estate. They are mostly male, except the tea pickers. Skipton's main business is in tea, but it has got many other domestic products. We are not involved with them but if you work in the head office you will be.

"Now I will delegate you some responsibilities once you get settled. I want you to look after the plantation site, particularly the production, delivery and quality of the product. We have a labour officer who looks after the wellbeing of the workers and the families of the employees, and as you know we have a doctor and compounder with outpatient facilities. Also, we run a small school.

"You will be able to supervise these things, not as part of your job but as a social enterprise. You will have enough help, but for the time being I will call somebody to take you around the estate.

Mr Malone called for Mahesh *Babu* to come in. Mr Malone told him: "This is Ashok *Babu*, your boss." Looking at Mahesh, he said: "Mahesh *Babu* will be your assistant." Both said "*Namaste*" and said good wishes to each other.

Mr Malone added: "I am going to write an official letter to each employee about Ashok *Babu*'s joining the firm, but in the meantime Mahesh *Babu* can take you around and introduce you to everybody."

Mahesh *Babu* was a short, small gentleman wearing a shirt and *dhoti*, with rimless glasses. He looked more of an intellectual. He said to Ashok: "Sir, I will call you Baro *Babu* – that will be better in introducing you to everybody."

Ashok jokingly asked: "What do you call Mr Malone then?"

Mahesh smiled: "We call him Baro *Sahib*."

Both came out of the office of Mr Malone. Mahesh *Babu* took Ashok to the middle of the office and Mahesh shouted: "Excuse me, quiet for a minute, I am going to introduce you to your new boss. This is Mr Ashok Banerjee. We will call him Baro *Babu*."

Everybody came with folded hands, bowed in front of Ashok and introduced themselves one by one. Ashok said: "Don't worry, I will come myself to each of you and introduce myself and have a chat with you privately."

Mahesh bought Ashok outside and said: "Can you see the two big ponds? We cultivate fish for ornamental reasons and also for catching, but Mr Malone doesn't like people catching the fish. We have two people to look after these ponds. You see the big garden and many beautiful flowers? They are looked after by two of the gardeners."

He called them over and introduced them to Ashok. Both bowed and welcomed Baro *Babu*.

Mahesh took him to the small dispensary and introduced Ashok to the compounder, Dr Singh, a gentle Nepalese man who had once been in the British army. He said unfortunately Dr Singh was not in today because he had gone to the village, but he would make sure Dr Singh came to see Ashok personally.

Mahesh very proudly said they looked after most illnesses and injuries among staff, but if anything serious happened they had a van to take people to the main hospital in Darjeeling. They were walking through the manicured marbled path of the Skipton building when an elderly man from the plant, with another middle-aged man, came running with folded hands.

Before Mahesh *Babu* could say anything, the middle-aged man said: "Baro *Babu*, I am the head of plantation and my name is Bansilal." This was the man who kept everything under control. He knew everybody's ins and outs, he kept a rota of all the plantation employees and knew who did how many hours and where they worked. And after the tea leaves were plucked, Bansi and his assistant weighed them, and men and women were paid according to the weight of leaves they picked.

Ashok said to Bansi: "It was a pleasure meeting you. It seems you are a very important person in this plant." The four men started up the hill to walk through the plantation. From afar the hill and tea plants looked beautiful and you could see every few yards there was a lady with a basket on the back picking the ripe tea leaves. They were experts and they knew which to pick and which to leave.

The four men went to the tea depot, where the leaves were spread out and left to dry in the sunshine. The leaves were then cut into small pieces, weighed and put in small, square cardboard boxes to be transferred to the main depot in Calcutta, and from there all over the world, where it was known as Darjeeling tea.

After a quick tour, Ashok thanked them all and then came back to his office with Mahesh *Babu*. He met Mr Malone again, who said: "For today it may be enough, but you organise your office and tell the boys what you need – they will sort it for you." Ashok said he had to sort out his house too; Mahesh stood and came with him to the main gate to see how he was getting home.

Malone said he could call the driver with the jeep to take him home, but Ashok said that was not required. He started walking and said goodbye to Mahesh. By now, Ashok knew the hilly roads to his bungalow.

He went home and told Ramu how to organise the bedroom better. Ramu asked how his first day had been. "Excellent," said Ashok. He had dinner and went to bed to read the contract of the job, which he hadn't read properly so far.

The following morning, Ashok again woke up a bit early, did his rituals and had breakfast and walked to the office at about half-past seven. Everyone stood up to say good morning and Ashok said: "That's fine. Please be seated."

Malone came in at about eight o'clock and called Ashok to his office, where he explained in as much detail as he could how the business worked. He talked about the profitability of the company, how much went out in wages, and how much was spent on the social affairs of the employees. Head office was always very keen to maintain the quality of the product. It couldn't slip. It also wanted profitability to go up year by year – the pressure was now on Malone and Ashok.

Ashok was a very sharp, intelligent man. It was not difficult for him to grasp what was required of him, but for his first job at least Mr Malone was there, and he said all along to seek his advice.

Mr Malone said: "Ashok, this Christmas I need to go back to England and I need at least two months off. From Calcutta to Southampton takes three weeks. You and I both can't be away at the same time, so make sure that you are here for these two months."

Ashok was thinking he should buy a cycle, because walking in a hilly area was not always fun. He also told Mahesh *Babu* that if anybody needed help in English he would be more than happy to help.

In the next few weeks Ashok wrote letters to Adi and uncle Dhruva and to his surprise he got replies from both. He was very reassured and happy reading those letters. It seemed Adi was happy living with his uncle and aunt. Ashok wrote to him about his new job, his new English boss and the Ambari people. He said they were very polite and honest.

He also said he had a big challenge coming when Mr Malone went away and Ashok would have to run the show. Adi wrote to say he was very confident that if anybody could do it, Ashok could. Ashok told Adi that as soon as he could manage some leave, he would definitely come and visit the village.

Ashok settled down in his job. Everyone seemed to like him as Baro *Babu*. Ramu was cooking very well. He got money every week for shopping and felt like a rich man as he went to the market often to buy whatever he needed.

One day Ramu said: "We need a new iron." But Ashok said: "You won't get one around here. You have to go to either Jalpaiguri or Siliguri."

Ramu said: "That's not a problem, I have been there once. With a new iron, I will be able to iron your clothes much better."

Winter came. It was a bit harsh, with north Bengal being so close to the Himalayas. The cold wind blew from the North and the daylight hours were very short. It got dark very quickly. You had to wear several layers of clothes, as well as a hat and scarves.

December came and Mr Malone said: "I am sure you will be fine running the show. If there is any problem, contact Mr Neil at head office."

Ashok and the driver came in the jeep to drop Mr Malone at Jalpaiguri station. Before going, Mr Malone hugged Ashok and said: "Look after the company well. They are already thinking of promoting you in a managerial post."

So Ashok became the de facto boss of the whole Skipton Industries operation in north Bengal. He worked very hard day and night and went to present his balance sheet to headquarters in Calcutta. They were very impressed that profits had gone up. The company director wrote him a personal letter thanking him and congratulating him for his magnificent work.

After two months Mr Malone came back and said: "I am glad you have done so well - now it's your turn. You could take a break, but I will tell you something very privately which I told Mr Neil – please don't tell anybody else.

"Back in England I have a lot of responsibilities. I have an elderly mother who needs looking after. I told the Company that after the financial year I will go back to England. I will be very sad to leave but it has to be done."

Ashok said: "What happens to your job?"

"Don't worry," he said. "I will get a job in England. I've had the time of my life in India, but it's time to move on. But I have recommended your name for my post. Let's wait and see."

When the time came and Mr. Malone packed up and went to London, Ashok came with the driver to drop him at Jalpaiguri. He packed all his bags. There was a young lady standing at the hill too, who was wiping away tears. Mr. Malone said: "Ashok, this is Phulan. She used to look after me. I told her that if she has any problem, to come to you. Please help the girl if needed." Ashok said: "No problem."

After a few weeks he was summoned by Mr Neil to come to the head office in Calcutta, which he did. Mr Neil said: "You are doing an excellent job. You could take this as an informal interview, but I called you to take it forward. If you are happy, we will make you the manager from the first of next month. Your salary and perks will go up. I am confident you will do a great job. So, Mr Banerjee, you are the general manager now."

Ashok became very busy, but the added responsibilities of the position gave him higher status in the whole of Ambari. After a month he decided to go to his home village, but only for a week or so because he could not stay away from work too long.

He gave some money to Ramu and said: "Tomorrow I will be going to Sukhobaspur – look after the place."

The following morning, Ramu brought the luggage to the jeep. He said he would come to Jalpaiguri and return with the driver. Ashok went straight to the village via the same route he had taken many times. He decided not to disturb Bishwanath this time.

He left his luggage at Sealdah, went to Harrison Road and had dinner and bought some gifts for Adi and aunt Bina. He stayed in a bed and breakfast and told them his train was at 10 o'clock but that he wanted a place to rest for the day. The owner gave him a room and said he could make any food he needed. "Just wake me up at five o'clock," he said.

At five o'clock he woke up. He had needed the rest. Ashok spoke to the manager over a cup of tea. They discussed the tension between the two religious groups in the east of Bengal.

Ashok said: "Our property is surrounded by Muslim people, but they are very nice. We have known them for generations. There were a few small troubles but that has calmed down."

At half-past five Ashok started walking towards Sealdah station. He bought a book of Sarat Chatterjee from the station bookstall. He boarded the train, went straight to his sleeper and started reading.

He arrived in Dhaka early on a pleasant, bright and sunny morning. His only problem was carrying all the luggage and presents he'd brought to the Dhaka port.

Ashok got on the steamer. It was supposed to start at 11 o' clock but for some reason it was running late. He managed to get a seat in the corner. He was very excited, very emotional and looking forward to seeing Adi. He enjoyed the scenic beauty while a musician sang a joyful song.

As Ashok left the steamer, to his surprise he saw Adi running towards him. Adi said: "I knew you would be coming around this time."

Ashok said: "How did you know I was coming today?"

Adi said: "From your last letter I got a hint that you might turn up this week, so, I dragged uncle Dhruva with me."

Ashok touched Dhruva's feet. Dhruva said: "God bless you. It's so nice to see you. So, how long are you going to stay with us?"

Ashok said: "Not very long. A few days."

Dhruva said: "Instead of opening up your house, I have asked Abdul to clean up our guest room for you to stay. But at the end of the day, it's your choice."

Ashok said: "What did aunt Bina say?"

Dhruva said: "She will be delighted."

After walking through the village roads between the paddy fields, Ashok was delighted. He could smell his hometown. Soon they arrived outside Dhruva's house and Dhruva shouted: "Bina, come out and see who is here."

Bina came out with Rahimi, one of the ladies who worked in the house. They were landless and had no money – one of her brothers, Akbar, had gone to Dhaka and started a business in shoes. It seemed he was doing well – Hindus don't work in the animal leather business.

The money to start the business had been given to Akbar by Dhruva.

He'd come back the previous year to repay him, but Dhruva refused to take it, saying: "Akbar, you are like my own family. So long as you look after your family and are doing well, I am happy."

Akbar wanted to take Rahimi to the city but Rahimi seemed to be happy working in Bina's house. Ashok touched aunt Bina Aunt's feet. Rahimi said: "Ashok, you look like a big boss now, but you lost a lot of weight."

They took Ashok's luggage to the guest room. Ashok opened the box and opened up all the presents he had brought. In the evening there was a big feast cooked by Bina and Rahimi. Then Ashok went to Adi's bedroom and had a long chat with him. It seemed Adi was very happy that he was staying with Dhruva and Bina and was doing better in his studies now. Ashok happily went back to his room and slept.

In the next few days he went around the village meeting several people. Over the weekend he booked a transport and took Adi to Radha's house. They were treated very well, but Ashok could tell that Radha was not very happy, and that she had been stopped from going out. He gave all the presents to Radha and left slightly bewildered as Radha kept saying: "Everything is fine. Don't worry about me."

They went back to Dhruva's house. At this time of the year there were lots of fruits and vegetables and an abundance of fish in the pond – so Bina cooked. In the evening he had a discussion with Dhruva, who said: "Ashok, if you are not coming back we have to have a plan for Adi.

"Although he has done well in school since you left, he is not a very academic boy. If you don't mind, I might train Adi to look after the farm. It's not a big holding but it will be enough for Adi and his family when we are gone and, as you know, the land-grabbing is going on here. And also, the Quit India movement has taken momentum.

"In a few years' time, with the religious tension around, I might not be able to look after the whole farm. Now, Abdul is there. He could teach Adi the trade slowly.

"At the present the British are running the country very well, but my worry is that if the British have to leave, they will divide Bengal in two and we might become a minority in our own ancestral land.

"And if they make Dhaka the capital of Bengal it will be difficult because there are more Hindus in Calcutta than in Dhaka. The latest census shows there are more Muslims in Noakhali and Barisal. The way the riots are progressing, I worry."

Ashok said: "You are very passionate about the whole issue. Don't worry, nothing will happen. We Hindus and Muslims have lived here peacefully like brothers and sisters for generations. Don't be so pessimistic."

Dhruva said: "I do really hope you are right, but I am really concerned."

Ashok stood up and said: "Don't be so pessimistic."

The weekend passed, and soon it was time for Ashok to depart to Ambari. Again, Adi and Dhruva came and dropped him at the steamer gate. Again, after a gruelling 18-hour journey, he arrived in Ambari – his car and Ramu both turned up.

Ramu very enthusiastically told him what exactly happened while he was away. Actually, nothing very much. Ashok came home and read the post. He had a letter from Mr Malone thanking him and hinting that he might not come back. He was planning to settle in the sunny south of France.

Ashok was becoming more and more popular around Ambari. He was asked to give sports prizes at the local club. He also went to a local school to give a talk about the importance of education, in particular promoting women's education.

A few weeks later, Ashok was working in his office when he heard a commotion between a lady and Mahesh *Babu*. The lady wanted to see Ashok *Babu* urgently but Mahesh said: "He can't see you today, he is very busy."

Ashok came out and saw a tribal, youngish and good-looking lady. Somehow or other, he thought he had seen this girl before. So Ashok invited her and Mahesh *Babu* in and closed the door.

"Have I met you before?" Ashok asked the girl.

"Yes," she said, "my name is Phulan. You saw me outside Mr Malone's house."

"I remember that. How can I help you?"

Phulan said: "I need to discuss something private."

Ashok said: "That's fine. But Mahesh *Babu* has to be here."

Phulan said: "I am pregnant."

Ashok said: "By whom?"

Phulan said: "By Mr Malone."

Ashok stood up. "Hang on a minute," he said. "Are you sure you know what you are saying?"

"Yes."

"Was there any force involved?"

"No, I used to love him."

"Did you tell him before he left that you are pregnant?"

"No, I did not."

"What do you want to do now?" asked Ashok.

Phulan said: "I want to keep the child."

"How long did you know Mr Malone?"

Phulan said: "My mother used to work in his house, but she had acute asthma and couldn't work. But we needed the money and my mother told me that Mr Malone was an excellent man. I went and worked for him, looked after him, cooked for him. He was a lovely man and I fell in love with him."

Ashok said: "I will go and talk to Mr Neil in Calcutta and take his advice. Does your mother know?"

"Yes, she sent me to you for advice."

"Do you realise that it will be a white child in a completely tribal area?"

Phulan said: "I don't mind that."

Ashok said: "Do you realise the difficulty the child will have?"

Phulan said: "I need a job."

Ashok said: "That's not a problem. I will organise a job for you here or in Calcutta." He told Phulan and Mahesh *Babu* the discussion should not go beyond that room, and that they would do whatever Phulan wanted.

The following week, Ashok made a special trip to Calcutta and telegraphed Mr Neil's secretary, saying that he needed to talk to him urgently. When they met, Mr Neil said: "I was very worried when they said you wanted to see me urgently. What's the matter?"

Ashok told him Phulan's story. Mr Neil was quiet for a few minutes. He said: "You know Ashok, this is not a new or isolated story. I deal with it every month. The solution is – and you can discuss it with the girl – that we will give her a job in the head office in Calcutta as a cleaner and our social service lead Mrs Vargis will look after her pregnancy.

"From the company we will organise a place near New Market where a large number of Anglo-Indian people live with their family. So this girl will not feel isolated and the child will get a good education.

"In the meantime, I will try to contact Mr Malone. Knowing the chap, he may not have any clue but then again, we may not find him. We will try to locate him and let him know. In the meantime, you could give 100 rupees to the girl for advance expenses."

The next week, Ashok called on Phulan and her mother with Mahesh *Babu* to tell them the plan. The girl was a bit worried about uprooting herself from tribal life to Calcutta, but she was reassured that Mrs Vargis from the company would look after all the eventualities. If that was not agreeable for her, things would become very messy. They asked for two days to think about it. When they came back, they agreed to the company plan. Mahesh *Babu* organised all the travelling and a place for her to stay when she arrived in Calcutta.

Ashok got a letter from Skipton's head office in London praising his hard work and management. The company's profit had gone up, so its shareholders were also happy. He informed Mr Neil that after a certain time he would like to come back to Calcutta in a managerial post. Also, he wanted to study for a BSc at Calcutta University.

Mr Neil wrote back saying he would be delighted and that, as soon as there was a vacancy in Calcutta, Ashok would be his first choice. Ashok was starting to feel a bit well off because his salary had gone up and because Ramu was cooking and looking after him so well.

Ashok also got a radio – but one day he became very upset and couldn't sleep because there was a big riot in the village next to his.

One afternoon a few months later, his office clerk came running to his house and said: "Baro *Babu*, there is an urgent telegram for you."

Ashok leapt up and opened the telegram as quickly as he could. It was a telegram from one of his classmates called Bijay. It said: "Riot everywhere, there is a big fire in your house. Come soon."

Ashok told the driver to bring the car as quickly as possible. He rushed to the office safe, where he used to keep his own money in a box. There was about 500 rupees from his salary. By now Mahesh *Babu* had arrived and Ashok said to him, the clerk and Ramu: "I have to go home. I will be back as soon as I can, but there seems to be a riot."

The driver took him to Jalpaiguri station, where the train was about to leave. He got a ticket and jumped on. There was no place to sit, so he had to stand for nearly eight hours. He came to Sealdah and from there took the East India Express.

He found a place to sit but the ticket collector said: "Sir, you are a Hindu

Brahmin - I wouldn't go to Dhaka if I were you."

Ashok said: "Why? How do you know I am Hindu?"

The man simply said: "There is a religious riot going on in Dhaka."

But Ashok said: "I have to go - my house has been set on fire."

The collector said: "Be careful, sir. I thought I should warn you."

Ashok couldn't sleep because he was so worried about what had happened to Adi and his uncle and aunt. He arrived at Dhaka station in the morning. There was a weary calm and a smell of burnt flesh and fire. Nobody was talking to anybody and there were soldiers everywhere. Everything looked very tense.

Ashok came out of the station and a police officer stopped him and asked to see his ID. When Ashok handed over his ID card, the officer said: "You are Mr Banerjee, the GM of Skipton Company. You must be a big shot. Why are you risking your life going to Sukhobaspur? You might lose your life."

Ashok said: "Sir, my brother is there. I need to go, come what may."

The policeman called his assistant and said: "Sultan Mia, Mr Banerjee has to go to Sukhobaspur. Can you escort him in one of our jeeps? He is a high-ranking officer for a British company."

Sultan Mia hesitated for a second and then said to Ashok: "I will take you, but don't say a word. I will talk on your behalf. I know your village well and I think I happen to know your family. I will talk to the police and the hooligans on the way.

"You are from this village, so you know the short cut. I will take two more police officers with me and you can guide us."

The jeep set off. Ashok couldn't believe his eyes. There were dead bodies all around the roads, houses half burned. You could still hear some women crying and you could smell burned flesh and blood everywhere.

Ashok's heart started pounding. He said to Sultan Mia: "I have got a young brother."

Sultan Mia said: "The thugs have killed everyone. Very few people have survived. You will be lucky if they are alive. I am just warning you. I have seen a few riots but this is the worst I have seen in my life."

Slowly they approached the village. There was a gang of youths standing on a corner with balaclavas on their heads and swords in their hands.

Sultan Mia said: "Why don't you guys go home and stop killing and maiming people?"

They barricaded the road and asked: "What's your name? Who is with you in the jeep?"

He shouted: "My name is Sultan Mia. I am the head constable. The men with me are all police officers."

They went on and Ashok approached his house. He couldn't stand - his house was burned, completely destroyed. He then ran to Dhruva's house shouting: "Adi, Adi, Adi."

Part of the house was burned and there was a lingering smell of flesh. Ashok couldn't believe what he saw, and he fell on the floor.

Sultan Mia said to him: "These are bastards. They don't belong to any religion. If I can catch them, I will shoot them."

He hugged Ashok and said: "It's getting dark here now. We have to go. I suggest you come and stay in our place or in a hotel in Dhaka. I can organise that. Tomorrow is my day off. First thing in the morning, I will pick you up and come back to the village again."

Ashok had no choice but to listen to Sultan Mia. He stayed in a hotel in the city, woke up at dawn and waited for Sultan to arrive. It was still early morning when they arrived at the village again.

Ashok was desolate and couldn't believe the massacre. He and Sultan

Mia went to Abdul's house. It was completely empty; it seemed people had left in a hurry.

A few hundred yards on, they came to Naseeb *Bhai*'s house. He had been working in the Banerjee family for generations. He hugged Ashok very tightly and started crying inconsolably.

Ashok asked Naseeb: "Who did this to us? We don't deserve this. And what happened to Adi?"

Naseeb stopped crying and said: "Most probably Adi has survived."

Ashok shook him and asked: "Where is he then?"

Naseeb said: "In the last few weeks the rumour was floating that Hindus were killing Muslims in droves in Howrah Bridge near Calcutta. When the news came, the young boys from the Muslim League at the mosque started planning some revenge attacks.

"Abdul heard about this and suggested Dhruva should move out of the house and go somewhere else, but Dhruva stoically said, 'These are all my own people. They won't do any harm to us'. But he agreed with Abdul that Adi would go and stay in his house in hiding during this tense period."

"Abdul had a small two-bedroom house at the end of the village and, although Adi was very reluctant, Abdul persuaded him to come and stay in his house at least for a few days. Abdul's wife and only daughter stayed in one room and they gave Adi Abdul's bed.

"Abdul came and stayed in Dhruva's house. In the middle of night about 10 or 12 mostly young people turned up, all wearing balaclavas. They looted the house and set fire to the property. Abdul recognised one of the boys - he was the son of a landless farmer who worked for Dhruva.

"Because Abdul told him, 'I know who you are', Abdul lost his life, as well as your uncle and aunt. This happened two weeks ago and after a few days I felt, as a life-long servant of your family, Dhruva *Babu* and his wife deserved a proper funeral. So I went with a few other guys from the village and cremated their bodies at the bank of Ganges in a proper Hindu ritual."

Ashok was shaking, and tears were rolling over his cheeks. "Then what happened to Adi?" he asked.

Naseeb said: "That's another story. After Abdul's death, his wife took their daughter and Adi and most likely went to Dhaka, where her brother has a garment business. But nobody is sure."

At least Ashok had some optimism that Adi had survived and felt confident that, given time, he would find him. With Sultan he went to the local *pandit*'s house and said: "Could you organise a proper *Shradha* of Dhruva and Bina Banerjee?"

The priest said: "Have they got any son?"

Ashok said: "I am their son."

After ten days he organised a proper Hindu ritual for his beloved uncle and aunt. There were few Hindus left in the village. He performed all the rituals a son is supposed to do.

Ashok sent a telegram to his headquarters that he would be a few days late in coming back. He went to the police station and filed a missing person's report for Adi with his description. The police wanted a picture, but all his pictures were burned.

Then, with Sultan Mia, he went to Dhaka again. He stayed in the Grand Hotel and started walking around all the garment factories and asking them about Adi, but nobody seemed to have any clue. Ashok looked very depressed, with an unshaven beard and uncombed hair. He looked like a shadow of himself.

Then somebody said: "If you go to Manik Bazar, you might get some answers."

But Sultan said: "Don't go there. You are a high risk. You might get killed there."

Ashok was adamant, he had to go and find Adi. By now he had not eaten for a few days. Sultan dragged him to his house. He said: "You have to come and eat, my wife will cook. Whatever happened, you can't reverse it."

But Ashok walked mile after mile, going north, south, east and west, wherever someone might have seen his brother, giving people a description of Adi.

Ashok didn't know what to do. He was lost and completely out of his mind. For the first time in his life, he couldn't think things through properly. He even ventured deep into the Muslim part of Dhaka, stayed at hotels there and went to all the mosques.

One guy said he knew a businessman called Shreeraj Hussain who ran a garment business. He could take Ashok there but it was a very risky place for him to go. Ashok went anyway, running a high risk that he would be detained, tortured or even killed. It seemed nobody had seen a boy fitting Adi's description.

Ashok informed the police again that he had to go back to work but would be back as soon as he could. He gave his address so they could send him a telegram if they had any news of his brother. Then, with a very heavy heart, Ashok went back to Ambari.

CHAPTER 9

Ashok went back to work. It was difficult to concentrate. It was impossible to forget what had happened. He kept thinking, did he make the wrong decision about Adi? Could he have done anything differently?

Three months passed with no news from the police or from the advertisement he had put in the newspaper. Not a single dot of information from anyone.

Ashok could not forget Adi's face. He wondered constantly where and how he was. In his mind, he was very sure his brother was alive.

A year passed and things became psychologically more bearable. Ashok went back to his village to do a one-year ritual for his uncle Dhruva and aunt Bina. He met lots of people, but he also found that lots of Hindu families had left the village.

Only one priest survived in the Kali temple. One of the reasons was that some of the Sufi Islam people used to come to the temple to sing. The priest organised a good ritual of commemoration. Ashok also invited a few people. He said that so far, he knew seven generations of his family had lived on this soil and he knew all their names.

After the ritual Ashok felt slightly more peace of mind. In the evening he was in the priest's house when the priest suddenly said to Ashok: "You need some healing touch. You are a young, educated man with a bright future. I think you have gone through a lot of bad times and it's high time that you get married. That will give you peace and stability."

Ashok said: "I cannot marry now unless I find out where Adi is."

Mr Chakrabarty said: "Listen, in the last five years 10 million Hindus have left home through ethnic cleansing, and who knows who went where. I am very confident your brother Adi is alive and may be doing very well. But you might not see him for 10 or 25 years. Of course, you will look for him, but while you are doing so you have to live life.

"The reason I mention marriage is that I have got a client, the richest land- owners in Bikrampur. They are Mukherjee Brahmins. Their elder daughter is called Tarini and she is a very good-looking, well-mannered and peaceful girl. I know her well. She would be a very good wife for a man like you."

Ashok said: "As I have nobody around, at the end of the day it will be my decision only."

Mr Chakrabarty showed him a black-and-white photograph of a young girl and said: "Look how beautiful she is."

Ashok had a quick look and said: "Yes, she is pretty."

Mr Chakrabarty said: "Shall I tell them about you?"

Ashok said: "I suppose you can."

The following day, Ashok left for his job. By now he was earning a very good salary as the General Manager of a British firm. He also had a provident fund and life insurance.

Ramu was running Ashok's life now. He did lots of shopping, cooking and cleaning and Ashok was happy with that and didn't interfere.

Ashok was informed that Phulan had given birth to a boy in Calcutta. He was completely white. It seemed Phulan was happy and she got a monthly salary from the company. Everybody knew she had an English child.

Ashok was getting busier every day but, at the back of his mind, the only thing bothering him was the whereabouts of Adi. He came to the conclusion that he was alive somewhere in Dhaka. Ashok got an old picture of Adi from one of his friends and this time he put it in the newspaper with the ad.

He got a letter from Mr Chakrabarty, the priest in his village, saying that the Mukherjees were very interested to talk to him regarding their daughter.

Ashok replied: "I need to come back to the village to re-energise the search for Adi."

Mr Chakrabarty replied that Ashok could come and stay with his family. They would be delighted if he did and he would inform the Mukherjees at the same time.

Taking leave for Ashok had become a big issue and he was keen to appoint an assistant as soon as he could. He informed his head office he was taking one week's leave and he turned up at Mr Chakrabarty's house.

Mrs Chakrabarty was delighted to see him and Mr Chakrabarty said: "While you are here, for a day we could go to Mr Mukherjee's house and you could see the girl also."

Ashok was more interested in going around his village and the neighbouring ones and asking each and every person about Adi. However, on the Monday Mr Chakrabarty took Ashok to Anand Mukherjee's house. It was about 20 miles away and they decided to take a boat and then walk the last five or six miles.

Anand Mukherjee was a big *Zamindar*. He owned a huge amount of land and was the biggest landlord in Bikrampur at the time. Ashok and Mr Chakrabarty arrived at the house, which was huge. It had three parts and a large garden in the front with lots of chairs and tables. Anand came out and Mr Chakrabarty said: "Sir, this is Ashok, about whom I have spoken to you a few times."

Anand was very hospitable. He immediately invited them into the house and they sat and had some general discussions. Ashok was a bit nervous and a little overwhelmed at meeting such a powerful man.

Anand tried to make him at ease, asking him to say something about himself. Ashok said he was 28, and had achieved a distinction with first class in matriculation. He was working with Skipton, a British company, as a general manager in Ambari in the north of Bengal.

"Who is at home?" asked Anand. Ashok was silent, then said: "Nobody."

"What do you mean? You haven't got any family?"

Ashok said: "My parents died during the smallpox epidemic. We had a small holding and my uncle used to do the farming. But, during the last riot he and my aunt were killed."

Anand said: "I am very sorry to hear that."

Ashok said: "I have got a blood sister, she is married into the Mukherjee family. Also, I have got a younger brother called Aditya. He is missing and I am looking for him."

Anand *Babu* said: "I don't get it. What do you mean, missing?"

Ashok said: "I will need some help from you to trace him. During the last riot, he was staying with a Muslim family who were very close to us. The man of the house was killed, so his wife has taken my brother and her one daughter to the city of Dhaka, where her brother lives.

"I am sure they will look after him well, but I did try to locate him. But Dhaka is such a big city and there are some parts which are no-go areas."

After they had freshened up, Anand invited them for lunch. They sat around a large table with shining cutlery. The maidservants brought the food but Anand's wife Lakshmi and Malati served Ashok. There was lots of food - it was a feast.

After the big meal, Anand said: "We have kept a room ready for you, so you can go and rest and when the sun goes down, we will sit on the porch."

There was a beautiful bed and Ashok lay on it but couldn't sleep. Time passed slowly. At about five o'clock they were summoned to the porch - it was in the open air under a tree - where Anand was sitting in a big armchair, with eight or nine chairs around and some small tables.

Anand said: "Come and have a seat. Did you sleep?"

Ashok said: "No, I was just lying and thinking about things."

But Chakrabarty *Babu* said: "Oh, I had a good sleep."

They were given mango juice. Lakshmi came and joined them. After a few minutes passed Ashok looked around and suddenly saw Malati was bringing a young girl by the elbow towards them.

Anand said: "Ashok, this is my only daughter Tarini."

Ashok looked up to see Tarini's face but she was looking at the floor. In the afternoon sunset and the gentle breeze, Tarini was wearing a red sari and a red blouse.

She looked simply stunning. Ashok was completely bowled over. This was the first time he had looked at Tarini. She was holding a plate with some sweets on it. Ashok had difficulty moving his eye away from Tarini's face.

Suddenly Mr Chakrabarty said: "Ashok, do you want some sweets?"

"Yes please," said Ashok and he took two sweets from Tarini's plate on to his plate. Tarini was still standing and Anand said to her: "Have a seat." Quietly, she sat down.

Anand said to Ashok: "Do you want to ask her anything?"

Ashok became a bit shy and said: "Not really."

Anand said: "In that case, Malati, you can take Tarini inside the house. Come, Ashok, I will show you part of our farm."

They walked to the front of the farm, which was huge. There was no end of cattle, and quite a few ponds. Anand said: "If you want to see more of my farm, Narayan can take you around."

Ashok said: "No, I think we should go back now. It's getting dark and we have a 20-mile journey home."

Anand said: "That's fair enough. Now I'd better make a direct point.

We like you and we have enquired about you. We will be glad if you agree to marry my daughter. Then we will discuss it further in future. You don't need to tell me now."

But Ashok said: "I have got nobody to discuss about my marriage and Mr Chakrabarty has told me all about you and Tarini. So from my side, it will be a privilege to marry your daughter."

Anand gave a big smile and hugged Ashok. Chakrabarty *Babu* was also very pleased. They departed for home.

From the following day onwards, Ashok went to every part of his village and neighbouring ones with an old picture of Adi – but it came to nothing.

Mr Chakrabarty told Ashok that Anand *Babu* was very keen for the marriage to go ahead in the winter, maybe December or January. He added: "Before you leave for Ambari, Anand is only 26 miles away from us. We could go one afternoon and finalise everything."

Ashok realised that arranging marriages was Mr Chakrabarty's job, that was how he supported his family. So he agreed. About a week later they turned up at Anand's house.

Anand said: "If you are happy, because you have no family of your own, I will organise the marriage in my estate."

"That will be a very good idea."

"Not only is Tarini my eldest, she is my lucky daughter and I will be quite happy to give you some land and a house for your marriage gift."

Ashok said: "No, that's not required because I won't be living here. I want to do graduation in the next two years and I have already got land - it's lying empty."

Anand said: "Do you mind giving me the sizes of your clothing so my tailor can make the wedding clothes for you and the friends who will come with you?"

Ashok said: "Nobody actually, but I have a young, energetic servant called Ramu – he will be coming. Maybe one or two other people will come all the way from Ambari."

While Ashok was coming out, Narayan stopped him and said Tarini wanted to ask him something. Ashok felt very nervous. This was the first time he actually saw Tarini; she was very fair, and she had big eyes.

She came and said to Ashok: "Thanks very much," then disappeared. Ashok wanted to say something but, before he could compose himself, Tarini was gone.

The following day he went back to work via Calcutta and Jalpaiguri. He told Mahesh *Babu* and his secretary he would be off for the whole of December. Mahesh scratched his head and said: "Baro *Babu*… for a whole month?"

"Yes," said Ashok. "I am getting married."

His secretary suggested: "In that case, you could move into the big bungalow from now on."

Ashok replied: "I don't think my wife will come to Ambari straight away."

He started enquiring about a BSc course in Mathematics from Calcutta University and waited to see whether he would be allowed to study in Ambari, or would have to wait for a transfer to Calcutta.

Ashok told Ramu about the marriage. Ramu got very excited and said he would definitely come with him. He immediately asked for some money so that he could get a new *dhoti* and *kurta* stitched and to get proper shoes. After all, it was his *Babu*'s marriage – he had to look good.

In the last week of November, Ashok and Ramu came to Mr Chakrabarty's house. Bishwanath and Manik turned up too; of course, Mr Chakrabarty knew that Ashok would pay him handsomely.

Anand organised Tarini's marriage very well. Narayan and Anup and Aakash all worked with a lot of enthusiasm and outside the garden they put up a huge *pandal* and a platform for the marriage ceremony. There was a temporary kitchen cooking for almost everybody from the village. Ashok and his few friends came from his original village and stayed in the Mukherjees' outhouse. Lakshmi called in the goldsmith and made lots of gold chains, bangles and a large number of gifts.

The marriage was conducted in Sanskrit. The festival went for at least seven days, with lots of music and dance, and was a very happy occasion. Ashok stayed two weeks and it was decided that Tarini will stay with her parents for the time being. Ashok gave Tarini a nice gold ring.

The whole village people thought that they looked well matched - a perfect couple. Ashok was six feet tall with wide shoulders and was slightly darker in complexion. Now he wore a new moustache and, in his new Punjabi and *dhoti*, he looked a very handsome man. On the other hand, Tarini was five feet tall and very slim, with a milk-like complexion. With a red Banaras silk dress and *sindoor* on her forehead, she looked the perfect Indian wife.

Two weeks passed very quickly. Ashok told Tarini everything about his life, his job, and his hunt for his brother, Adi. Ashok promised to write her a letter as soon as he arrived at Ambari.

So Ashok and Tarini started their married life – but for the time being they had to stay separate because Ashok had to go back to his work.

PART THREE

CHAPTER 10

Ashok went back to work and, as promised, he wrote a letter once a week to Tarini. He was not a very good writer, but he told her all about his job, its difficulties and the food Ramu was cooking – and told Tarini to look after her health. He also passed on the good news that he had managed to appoint an assistant. Once this man settled in, maybe in a couple of months, Ashok would be able to come back home.

He had started calling Tarini's house his home because he had no home left of his own. He also had got a good salary now, so he was saving some money. He felt he had done as much as was humanly possible about Adi, but he was an optimistic man and he felt sure he would find his brother pretty soon.

Ashok's job had become much easier because he had become good at dealing with difficult decisions, and at man-management. He travelled to Calcutta to meet his director, Mr Neil, who seemed very happy with his performance. He also congratulated him on his marriage. Ashok said he would like whenever possible to get a transfer to the head office in Calcutta because he wanted to complete his university course. He was also keen to bring Tarini to Calcutta.

Mr Neil reassured him that as soon as there was a vacancy, he would call Ashok for an interview. He also said: "Only a very small handful of people do graduation. With your qualifications you could go up to the top of the company."

After a couple of months, Ashok came to stay in his in-laws' house. It was a bit embarrassing to stay for two weeks but he had no choice. He was looked after well, but he was surprised to see Anand *Babu* looking somewhat gaunt. Ashok enquired after his health and Anand said he was not sure, but he was losing weight and his stomach always felt full. He had consulted the village doctor, who gave him a few medications, but they had made no difference.

Ashok said: "There is a top English doctor in Calcutta who is a friend of Mr Neil. I can make an appointment through Mr Neil and take you to see this doctor."

Because Ashok had two weeks in hand, he did manage to get an appointment with Dr Mills in Calcutta. He did multiple tests on Anand and said: "He must have a lump in his stomach. It could be a growth and the prognosis may not be bright."

Ashok and Anand came back disappointed, but Anand took it very philosophically. Anand said, holding Ashok's hand: "I know myself. I am not going to make it very long, and I am very glad to get a son-in-law like you. When I am gone, Narayan is only 18 and Anup and Akash are very young. They will need your help."

Ashok reassured him. After two weeks Ashok had to go back. Tarini wanted to come up to Dhaka to see him off with Narayan, but Ashok thought that might not be a good idea.

A few months passed and Ashok received a letter from Tarini that said Anand's health was very poor. He was struggling to walk even a few steps and was often breathless. Ashok wrote back that because of the pressure of his job, it would be impossible for him to come.

However, he said that his friend Bishwanath knew a top surgeon in Calcutta. He would make an appointment and Narayan could take Anand to see Mr Chatterjee, the surgeon at Calcutta Medical School.

It was a long journey in the car. Bishwanath went with them. They went to Esplanade, the neighbourhood where all the doctors' chambers were. Anand looked very ill and was exhausted.

Dr Chatterjee examined him thoroughly and he told Bishwanath he would do some blood tests and a barium meal in the Presidency General Hospital - he would see Anand two days later with the results.

Anand and Narayan stayed in the Grand Hotel, at the heart of Esplanade near the surgery. After two days they went back with the blood and X-ray plates. Dr Chatterjee explained there was a large tumour in the stomach and it had spread to the chest as well. It was inoperable.

Bishwanath went privately to have a chat with Dr Chatterjee and asked him: "What is the prognosis?"

Dr Chatterjee said: "Maybe six months. Take him home and look after him. Make sure the local doctors control his pain."

Anand came back with Narayan. Tarini decided to look after her ailing father. Ashok managed to come for a few days to make sure Anand was comfortable and well looked after. This time Tarini came to the steamer station with Narayan to wave him goodbye.

Before leaving, Tarini said: "Whatever happens, I want to look after my father."

Ashok said: "That's fine by me, but this time I may not be able to come for six months or so."

Tarini asked: "What about our marriage anniversary?"

Ashok said: "There is a delegation from Skipton coming from London to visit our estate, I cannot leave at this crucial time."

He put quite a few rupees in Tarini's hand and said: "Look after yourself but if anything drastic happens to your dad, I will definitely try to come for a day or two. It will be hard, but I will try."

Ashok's steamer hooted and started moving. Tarini was standing on the bank with Narayan, tears flowing from her eyes.

Ashok arrived back at work to find his desk full of papers. Mahesh *Babu* came and asked him to sign lots of documents. He talked to as many people as he could and told them about the impending visits.

The following day, he sat with all the accountants and had to decide about the bonus during *Durga Puja*. Because the profit had been less this year, he had to tell all the employees their bonus would be smaller. He needed to talk to as many people on the farm to explain the difficulty with the finance.

The political situation of the country was not good. There was unrest everywhere for a variety of reasons. The biggest one was religious; the Muslim League and Congress couldn't agree and it seemed that partition in future might be the only option.

A huge riot took place in Calcutta that killed hundreds of Muslims and some Hindus. The British ambassador and the home minister tried to calm things down but it took several days. At the end, the army was called on to the street to impose calm.

Three months later, Ashok was working in his office when a *peon* knocked and said: "Baro *Babu*, you have got a telegram."

Ashok opened it and, as he feared, it was a telegram from Narayan saying that Anand *Babu* was in the terminal stage and asking him to come soon. Ashok called his PA, Binay *Babu*, grabbed a few things and said: "I have got this telegram. I have to go - I will be back as soon as I can."

He called the driver, took some of his money from the safe and said: "Let me go home first to get some clothes, then you can drop me at the rail station." He went home, told Ramu he had to go and would be back as soon as he could, then took a train and rushed back to Dhaka.

He arrived outside the Mukherjees' house unshaven and unkempt. Everything was quiet and deadly silent. Outside Anand's bedroom, Narayan was standing and weeping bitterly. He hugged Ashok and said: "You are too late. Dad passed away in the early morning. I am going to call the priest and organise the cremation rituals."

Ashok entered the room. Anand, looking like a skeleton, was lying peacefully with Lakshmi and Malati sitting on either side and Tarini at the foot of the bed, sitting on the floor.

Hindus cremate bodies before sunset because the body starts getting rigor mortis after a few hours - and the daytime heat makes it worse.

Anand left behind two wives, Lakshmi and Malati, and three sons: Narayan (18), Anup (14) and Akash (10) - and Tarini. Ashok entered quietly and said: "At least he died peacefully. I had better go now with Narayan to sort out the rituals."

Anand *Babu* had been a prosperous landlord. Slowly the news spread all around the village and a large gathering of people turned up, all saying what a good master he was.

They put him on a small *Khatiya*, a wooden platform with a mattress. Some people cleaned his body with perfumes and the body was covered up to the neck while the head and the face were decorated with sandalwood paste. Many flowers were put on him and a few garlands around his neck.

All four bearers were wearing *dhotis* with their sacred thread on and were bare-footed as they carried the body on the *Khatiya* towards the bank of Ganges. They kept reciting Sanskrit *shlokas* from the *Gita*. Behind, all the ladies hugged each other and cried - women were not allowed to come to the cremation ground.

A cremation pyre was made and lots of sandalwood was put on the body. The priest kept chanting hymns and Narayan put the fire to the cremation pyre. Once the cremation was finished, they took the ashes to the Ganges and walked home in bare feet. After 10 days people were called to pray for the deceased person and have some food, which they did in a big way.

Ashok had very limited time but he had to sort out all the logistics. Narayan was over 18, so technically he could be the owner of the whole estate. But Ashok took him to a lawyer and made sure all the paperwork was done, so Narayan became legally the owner of Anand's estate.

Then Ashok had to leave. Although he and Tarini had been married for more than a year, the circumstances were such that they had to live apart. While he was in Dhaka, Ashok again made a lot of enquiries about Adi, but drew a blank.

In Ambari, Ashok bought a new Raleigh bicycle. He liked exercise, so he went everywhere on his shiny new cycle. He also wrote to Tarini that she should keep a full-time maid for herself and Ashok would pay for it, so that she could fulfil all her requirements.

The weather had been dry for two successive seasons. But the monsoon was terrible and it ruined a lot of crops. Many houses had been swamped. There were no crops and in some parts a famine had started. The workers were getting very worried because the prices of food and vegetables had gone through the roof.

He reassured the workers that he would go to head office and request a pay rise for the workers. Calcutta was suffering from famine and cholera, but Ashok decided to go to the city.

There were lots of beggars in the street. This was the first time he had seen many people dying of starvation - there were bodies everywhere. It was a bad time. Mr Neil was very sympathetic, but he said the company finances were very tight and he could not agree to a pay rise.

However, he said to Ashok: "I am going to London in a few weeks' time. When I come back I will be able to get you to Calcutta as my assistant. It will be a promotion with lots of responsibilities. So, wait for that."

Ashok came back empty-handed, but he reassured everyone that he was trying his best. Under the circumstances they should keep their heads down and wait for better times to come.

Ashok wrote to Tarini saying it was likely that in six months' time he would get a promotion to a regional manager job in Calcutta. He was in two minds. He saw some houses in Ambari and debated whether to bring everything to Ambari and after a few months transfer them to Calcutta, or to go to Calcutta in one go.

Tarini was very disappointed but also delighted that her husband would get another promotion. Everyone looked after her very well at home, but that was beside the point.

Ashok bought lots of books for Tarini and she read them. She was not very keen on cooking and left it to her mother, but she had picked up some knitting and also did crochet. Narayan was looking after the business with the help of his father's assistants.

On the other hand, Anup and Akash were not very keen on studies. In their spare time they helped Narayan but they were keen on going out and enjoying themselves.

After a couple of months, Ashok came and stayed for a couple of weeks. It was becoming a ritual for him to make the journey, which altogether took 18 hours. He didn't mind. He was very sure this would finish very soon. While he was home, he discussed a few things with Narayan and helped him to understand the business better. After all, Ashok had been running a bigger business for some years now.

He sent a monthly money order to Tarini so that she didn't need to ask for anything from anybody. But for a month he didn't receive any letter from Tarini. It was bitterly cold.

As per the company protocol, he moved to a bigger bungalow on a hilltop where Mr Malone used to live. At last he got a letter and he was delighted and excited to read that Tarini was expecting a child. Ashok immediately told her to get the best midwife. He sent some money and told her that within a couple of months he would be there.

The time did not pass quickly enough, but he got slightly anxious because he didn't receive a letter from Tarini. He wrote another letter and sent more money. He was trying to take time off, but it was getting impossible. He started organising the new bungalow, thinking that Tarini would be able to come once the baby was born.

After receiving no reply, Ashok decided to go home for three days. The journey was fine, but when he arrived Narayan was waiting for him outside the house looking down and quiet.

Ashok asked: "What's the matter? Is everything all right?"

Narayan said: "Come inside the house. We will talk."

Ashok realised something was not right. By now, at the sound of his voice, Tarini would have come out. He sensed something amiss. He went into their bedroom and found Tarini sitting on the corner of the bed with her head down. Ashok understood what had happened. He didn't need telling.

He went to Tarini to hold her and said: "I am very sorry. How are you?"

Tarini cried and said: "I couldn't hold on to the baby. I had a miscarriage and it was a girl."

Ashok sat next to her and said: "What exactly happened?"

Tarini cried and said: "Nothing really. I had a tummy ache. I was reading a book. Suddenly I started bleeding profusely. Ma came and called the midwife. She told me it was a daughter. I couldn't hold her."

Ashok, lost for words, asked Tarini: "When did it happen?"

She whispered: "Two weeks ago."

Ashok said: "You should have told me. I would have come."

Tarini said: "You are so busy. I didn't want to bother you."

Ashok asked: "How are you feeling now?"

"I lost a huge amount of blood. But it is better now. My midwife told me to stay in bed and she organised a special diet for me so that I get stronger quickly. They are looking after me extremely well."

Ashok felt a huge sense of loss. He was devastated inside. He wondered if his decision to leave Tarini here had been the right one. He reassured Tarini and tried to boost her morale as much as he could.

Over the next few days he discussed matters with Lakshmi and Malati. They were also very upset. They had been looking forward to a grandchild but they reassured Ashok that they would make sure Tarini recovered fully from this disappointment.

Lakshmi also said they had got a cottage near the Ganges in a hill station. They might take Tarini for a few weeks to recover.

Narayan asked Ashok to come to his office to help him to make some difficult decisions. He wanted some help modernising his business.

Also, Anup and Akash were getting impatient because they didn't want to continue in their study - they wanted to join Narayan in the business.

They knew they were a family of a huge land-owning *Zamindars*, so they didn't need to look for a job, and even if they didn't work money would not be an issue.

On his journey back, Ashok stayed again in a Dhaka hotel for a night. He talked to all the contacts he had there but the only positive news the police could give him was that Adi left the village unharmed and went to Dhaka business district with a Muslim family. They don't know anything more than that about his whereabouts.

After all this bad news, Ashok decided to push for his Calcutta transfer as soon as possible so that he could bring Tarini there and lead a normal family life.

Back at work, there was a huge problem regarding the tea-picking girls. These girls were mostly tribal or mixed. They came from Nepal, Sikkim and Bhutan and many of them were mixed race with Bengalis. The clerks hired and fired these girls, who mostly came from poor backgrounds.

All day they picked the leaves and put them in the basket and in the evening a few workers with a big weighing machine would weigh the basket to see how much they had picked in the day. They were paid according to the weight of the basket. These girls' entire earnings and livelihoods depend on these few clerks.

These people were very keen to take back-handers or favours. Ashok was very naïve about it - he had not known anything about this.

In the tea field there were some gardens where the picking was much better than in others. The junior *Babus* would favour the girls who were happy to look after their needs.

One of the girls was targeted by an office clerk. She knew this *Babu* would want to have a drink in the evening and then want to be entertained. This girl was brave enough to come and see Ashok and tell him how she was being treated.

Ashok had never met this girl personally, she was one of about 500 ladies working there. He was staggered by the amount of exploitation going on. This girl had accepted this behaviour as normal, part of life and the job. Ashok called Mahesh *Babu* and said: "Can you call all the women to the assembly hall in the morning?"

The next morning, all the girls turned up. They were very frightened, worried what the boss was going to say. First of all, Ashok said how sorry he was to hear about the exploitation of the ladies - he was extremely sorry for that. From the next day, all the people hiring and firing the girls would be removed from their post.

He said: "You girls decide who are the two among you, who will be called captain and vice-captain, to play this role. We could do this by a show of hands and we will appoint them in this post for one year. After that, if they do the job well they should continue, or we will get another two."

The women immediately decided who would be their two leaders. Kamala and Sharla were the ladies who would be in charge of the hiring and firing of girls - with no men involved.

Ashok hadn't heard anything from Mr Neil. Maybe he was not back from London? Ashok was very keen to get his job transferred to Calcutta, even though he had come to like Ambari and the people there. He told Ramu that if he was transferred to Calcutta, Ramu could come with him and do the same job. Ramu was delighted with that.

The Ambari village people came to talk to Ashok. They wanted to make him the chairman for *Durga Puja*. This was the biggest festival in the village, when the whole farm was shut for the holiday.

The story is that the Goddess Durga, wife of Shiva, came to see her father with four children. The Hindus celebrate this as a festival of joy when Durga brings her children home. The eldest son Ganesh is supposed to give success in life. Second is the daughter Lakshmi, goddess of wealth. Third is the goddess Saraswati, for art, culture and education. The fourth is her son Kartik, the god of craft.

The festival goes on for five days. First you invite Durga and her family to come. Durga, who killed the demons and made the world free from evil. Then the celebration goes as follows: *Shasti* (the sixth day of the moon's cycle), *Saptami, Ashtami, Nabami and Dashami* (the day she goes back to her own home). It's a huge festival - people make big *pandals* and decorate the deities with a lot of flowers and sweets. Everyone in the village turns up to celebrate in new clothes.

Ashok was very flattered and agreed to the honour. He made a large contribution for the festival. He wrote to Tarini telling her what was happening and told her to take things easy. He also told her he would be back as soon as he could manage.

He also wrote a letter to Bishwanath saying that he would be in Calcutta the next month for a meeting. He would be staying at the Great Eastern Hotel because it was an official visit, and he invited Bishwanath to have dinner with him there on the Saturday. He also said that Tarini had knitted a jumper for Ashok as his birthday present. One of the men from the village worked in Calcutta and he might drop it into Bish's studio.

Ashok came to Calcutta for his meeting with Mr Neil, who had returned. When he arrived at the Great Eastern Hotel, he was very pleased to find he was given the president's suite for three nights.

The following morning Ashok, with his new clothing and new shoes, put some brylcreem on his hair and went straight to Skipton House. This time Mr Neil's secretary was a Goanese lady. She looked at Ashok and, before he could say anything, said: "I take it you are Mr Banerjee. Mr Neil is waiting for you in the director's office."

Ashok had brought all the papers in his briefcase, so they went through them for a couple of hours. Mr Neil ordered lunch for both of them and during the meal he said: "I am very pleased with your performance. The business is doing well, the profit is up and the productivity is also up.

"I would have liked to bring you to the Calcutta office but unfortunately, the appointment was not approved by the board of directors. But I am sure, given time, it will be approved. In the meantime, I can only increase your salary. But be assured, Mr Banerjee, we will make you Regional Manager very soon."

Ashok was happy with everything, but it wouldn't help him to bring Tarini as soon as possible. He came out of the office and took a tram to Bowbazar through the hustle and bustle of Calcutta. It was nearly dark when he arrived at the studio. Bishwanath jumped up and embraced Ashok, saying: "You look very smart. I am so delighted to see you."

He took the jumper from his bag, gave it to Ashok and said: "This is from Tarini, with love." Ashok immediately put it on.

Bishwanath said: "Fantastic. I just locked the studio but come in, I will take a picture and you can give it to Tarini as a present from me."

Bish asked where he was saying and couldn't believe it when Ashok told him: "The Great Eastern Hotel. I am on official duty, So the company keeps me in a five- star hotel. So, I am here to take you with me to have dinner there."

Bish said: "Are you sure?"

Ashok said: "One hundred per cent."

Bish said: "In that case I had better tell Manik to let my wife know I will be late tonight."

They walked to the hotel. Bish was very impressed and when he saw Ashok's suite, he couldn't believe how plush and impressive it was.

Neither Ashok nor Bish drank alcohol, so they decided to start with some juice. There was some India-made alcohol which comes from rice or dates, but most Indians didn't drink alcohol. Most of the Scotch and the French wine was kept for white Europeans.

Downstairs in the dining room, Ashok booked a table for two and asked Bish if he would like to have French cuisine. Bish said: "Why not?"

Over the French food they discussed sports, politics and the religious tension. Time passed very quickly. Suddenly Bish said: "I have to leave by 10 o'clock. My last tram leaves Dalhousie Square at exactly 10 o'clock and from the tram depot of Ballygunge my house is about a two-mile walk."

At nine o'clock Bish got up. Ashok said: "I will take you up to the tram station."

Bish hugged him and said: "It was so nice to see you and spend some time. You look like a boss nowadays. Next time, official or unofficial, when you come to Calcutta you are going to stay with us."

Ashok went to his room, had a shower and did his puja. He used to wear a sacred thread, and most Brahmins pray or do puja once a day. On the hotel pad, he wrote a letter to Tarini about his Calcutta trip, how good the jumper looked and what a great time he had with Bish. His next travel home would be in a few months' time because he had already exhausted all his annual leave. And the transfer to Calcutta seemed to be delayed again.

Although Tarini was feeling lonely, going to the bank of the Ganges for a few days has done her a lot of good. She was feeling much better, more energetic, and was trying to help both mothers with the household chores. Narayan's business was doing very well and he had been very helpful, always asking if Tarini needed anything.

Narayan was not a very sharp man but he compensated for that with his hard work. He had become a member of a shooting club run by English people. He bought some guns and took Anup and Akash with him. They also started going to the business and trying to learn how things were done.

But whatever Tarini said went. All three brothers were obedient and she was very pampered by them. Although a new law said an estate should be divided equally between men and women, Tarini was not interested in the property.

Narayan kept saying that everyone had an equal share in the land and the house, including her. But Tarini knew in her heart that as soon as Ashok settled down in Calcutta, she would go and stay with him.

Ashok kept sending money to Tarini by money order, even the village postman knew about it. Tarini did tell Ashok she hadn't spent any of the money he had sent before, so she didn't need any money at the present time. But Ashok told her to buy some presents on puja for her mothers.

Ashok also went to Ambari's main market with Ramu and bought some saris for Tarini, Lakshmi and Malati, and some gifts for Narayan and the other two brothers. At puja time he was planning to visit Tarini again, but Ramu insisted that he also wanted to come. So, Ashok organised tickets for both of them. He also took Ramu out for a meal in Harrison Road while waiting for the train.

He had two sleepers on the train. He told Ramu to sleep on the bottom bunk and he slept on the top. They arrived at Dhaka and then took the steamer to the other side. This time Tarini knew he was coming and when he came off the steamer he was surprised to see her and all his brothers-in-law standing outside for him. They knew about Ramu from beforehand.

Ashok started walking and talking to all of them. They had to walk very slowly because Tarini couldn't walk fast. Narayan started explaining how the business was going and Ashok asked whether he had implemented the advice he'd given him. Narayan said he had.

Then he told Ashok about the religious tension creeping up in this part of Dhaka, which had not been an issue before. By then they had arrived at the house. Ashok sat on a chair and Lakshmi gave him and Ramu gave him a glass of coconut water. She said: "You guys must be very tired. Have a swim in the pond, then we will have dinner together."

After dinner was over, Ashok took Tarini and went straight to the bedroom. The next day, Tarini cooked a few things especially for Ashok that he loved. He went for a sight-seeing cycle with all his brothers-in-law and Ramu. They rode up a lot of hills and the beautiful scenery was peaceful. He had a pleasant time.

He told Tarini he had an interview for the regional manager's job in Calcutta, so he needed to go back and prepare.

A few weeks later, Ashok was summoned for the interview to head office. Mr Neil was there and Mr McKenzie, one of the directors from London, was also on the interview panel. It was an informal meeting, but he was told they had decided to appoint him as regional manager for Skipton Industries. He would be based in Calcutta on a very good salary scale, but the job would start in the new financial year - in four months' time.

Ashok was ecstatic and he sent a telegram to Tarini saying: "Got the job. Will start in four months." Tarini also wrote back congratulating him and giving him the good news that she was pregnant again. Ashok wrote that this time she should have the best midwife, get plenty of rest and be as careful as she could.

Now the timing of the transfer to Calcutta could be very good. He could go and organise everything and by the time the baby was born they could all move to Calcutta together.

In the meantime, Ashok had another meeting in Calcutta. He met Bish and his wife and took them out for dinner. He also decided to see Tarini for a couple of days to keep her calm and ensure the pregnancy went well. When he went, Narayan said to Ashok: "Don't worry. We will look after Tarini well this time."

Tarini asked him why he couldn't take the Calcutta post earlier. Ashok explained the gentleman he was replacing, wasn't leaving for four months, so he had to wait.

This time Tarini's pregnancy was going much better. She was not sick any more and she was doing whatever the midwife said. And when Ashok went back via Dhaka, he went again everywhere he could to enquire about Adi.

CHAPTER 11

Winter was slowly creeping in. The sun stayed in the sky for a very short time these days and much of the time it was dark. Some mornings and evenings the wind chill was so bitter, a gust of wind would rattle your bones. Winter wasn't the most fun in this part of this world, but there was compensation in the colourful variety of food that is in abundance during the winter months. You get a mix of vegetables with brightly coloured fruits and an abundance of fish from the rivers and ponds.

People tended to go home earlier, following the setting of the sun. The usual meetings, gossiping and gatherings on the porch of every house became less and less frequent. There was a weary silence in the villages. The only noise you could hear was the crickets. Most of the villages were not densely populated and were small in number.

Interestingly, while the villages remained small, they were separated by people's occupation and, more recently, by their religion. For example, one village's name could be translated as Kumar's village. This was a village full of potters; people who made earthen pots and pans, cups and saucers and, during the festival months, Hindu deities.

To make the deities the villagers had to get a different kind of clay. They went in twos and threes to the middle of a river on a small boat. One of the party dived in with a bucket to the base of the river and collected clay. The bucket was small and he had to do it many times over. It was hard work. In those days there were no oxygen masks to dive deep in the water - these people's lung capacity must have been very good.

With this clay they mixed some sand and made a dough and from there, with their clever hands, they carved all the deities, put them in the sun and then on a burner. Then they painted them.

The next village might be houses of carpenters and builders. They made furniture not only from bamboo and coconut ropes, but also built houses from bamboo and tree trunks, with mud and straw.

Next could be a village of weavers. They had small handlooms and would make thread from cotton which they picked from the nearby cotton plant. They would then use this thread to make *dhotis and saris* with their handlooms. The work was mostly done by the women.

The winter months were big fun for children because the schools were closed for a month for the Puja festivals. Each night, in the centre of the village, there was a dance or drama show. These were usually religious and mythological stories – the *Ramayana or Mahabharata.*

People flocked together and sat on the ground around a circular stage made from connected wooden platforms, with a locally made carpet placed on top. The artists came from different villages, dressed up and wore multi-coloured costumes and masks. They would come out from a type of "green room" and act on the stage.

There would be some high-powered kerosene lamps around the stage called *hazaks*. They made things very bright all around. For important people there were a few chairs put at one end. There was always a comedic character who made the children laugh.

Tarini was thinking of going to Ambari this winter, even though she was pregnant. However, because of her previous history, and the fact she was getting a bit of back pain, the midwife suggested that she shouldn't travel. Ashok also thought this was a better idea. There was plenty of help around and Tarini needed to stay vigilant because of what had happened the last time.

The pregnancy was going smoothly enough. The expected date was not very far away but Tarini, understandably, was very apprehensive. One Sunday evening she started getting labour pains. The midwife was there, as were Lakshmi and Malati. They all gathered around Tarini. After midnight her pain became quite severe but by 3am Tarini delivered a healthy boy. Everybody was delighted. Lakshmi, Malati and all the ladies said: "The boy looks like his dad and he has beautiful eyes."

The custom in those days was for mother and baby to stay in the same room for 11 days immediately after birth. At this point, there was a small puja to mark the mother and child coming out of the room to show the child to the world. It was a custom born from practicality, due to the health risks in those days and the number of infant illnesses and deaths. Ashok was working when he got the telegram and he bought a huge amount of sweets to celebrate the birth of his son. He asked Mahesh to distribute sweets to the whole office, and to tell everybody that Ashok *Babu* had a son.

When Ashok arrived home, he was delighted to see mother and son doing so well. There is a naming ceremony in India, and the household was busily preparing for this. So, with the pressure on, Tarini asked Ashok: "What should we call our boy?"

Ashok said: "I've thought about it and I would like my son to be called Vikramaditya."

"Vikramaditya?"

"Yes, why?"

"It's very nice, but it's a bit too long and a bit of a tongue twister."

"OK," said Ashok. "In that case, how about Abhishek Banerjee?"

After a short pause, Tarini replied: "I like that. Have you thought about a nickname?"

"I will leave that to you."

Everybody around the *Zamindar*'s house was delighted. This was the first grandson in the family, although it was technically a Banerjee. Narayan organised a huge party and invited everyone from their village. It was a great success.

Ashok went to town with Narayan and bought lots of clothes for the baby and lots of saris for the ladies in the house. Narayan sent some sweets to all the relatives and distant relatives of the family with this good news.

Ashok went back to work and this time he told Mr Neil that if the Calcutta job was getting delayed, he might have to bring his family in Ambari and settle there until he got the transfer. "The other option, if you don't mind," he said, "is for me to apply to other jobs in Calcutta."

"There's no need to do that," said Mr Neil. "It's a matter of a few months." After a couple of months, he could go home and organise bringing Tarini and Abhishek to Ambari.

It took Ashok a month or so to organise the bungalow properly. Although it was a large one, it needed a baby cot. The kitchen needed revamping and they needed a king-sized bed. All were put in place.

After two months, Ashok and Ramu went to Tarini's house with lots of presents for everybody. They stayed there for a week or more and packed up whatever needed to be taken to Ambari. Ashok said not to take too much luggage because they could get almost everything for babies at the nearest town, Jalpaiguri.

Narayan organised a car to take them from their village all the way to Dhaka, so they wouldn't need to take the steamer and an overnight train journey but organising a car from Calcutta to Jalpaiguri was a different proposition. Bishwanath suggested that Ashok, Tarini and the baby went on the train. Ramu, Manik and two other guys from Calcutta would bring their luggage in a day or two. Ashok thought that was a better idea.

Tarini was excited and delighted with the beautiful bungalow they had on the hilltop and she decorated the baby's bed with colourful toys all around, some of them musical. Slowly but steadily, with the help of Ramu, she put the house in order. It had been a bachelor's pad but it became a beautiful home.

Ashok became as busy as one could be with his job and he was getting involved more and more with social activities. Ramu was cooking all sorts of exotic food for his *Bhabhi* including making some traditional tribal food. However, there was a limit because Tarini was totally vegetarian.

They got some things like milk, eggs and bread delivered at home by the milkman and the vegetables were also delivered to the door by some vendors but if she needed, she could go to the village market in Ashok's jeep. They also appointed a middle-aged lady to look after Abhishek so Tarini could get some rest.

Everybody said Ashok was putting on some weight because he was being looked after very well. They were having a pleasant young family life and Abhishek was now a few months old. Ashok took a call from the head office to tell him his job as a regional manager would start in six months' time. He got the appointment letter.

Ashok and Tarini were delighted. They discussed what to do. Ashok suggested that, a couple of months before his transfer, he would take Tarini and Abhishek to her mother's house for a month, so that he could commute to Calcutta and organise a decent house for them to live and. They would take Ramu and the lady with them. Tarini agreed.

About a month later, Ashok made a work trip to Calcutta and stayed in a hotel. While he was there, he took Bish to see some houses in the south of Calcutta. One house he liked was in Ballygunge. It had four bedrooms, a garden in the front and back, and a good kitchen. The rent was a bit high but now Ashok was in the executive salary bracket it should not be a problem.

Bish said: "You could get a tram from outside your house directly to your office. On a good day, you could even walk to your office." Also his evening assignments at the University wouldn't be a problem. Overall, Ashok was very excited and he put down an advance deposit to book the house.

He went back and told Tarini, who said she would be happy wherever Ashok was happy. Ramu got very excited because, being a tribal boy, he had never been to Calcutta.

Ashok and Tarini decided their plan and wrote a letter to Narayan explaining that they would live in Calcutta, but that for a month Tarini and Abhishek would stay with him while Ashok went back to Ambari to wind up his old job - although technically, in his new role he would still be boss of the estate.

The monsoon was pretty bad this year. In June and July, there is a depression in the atmosphere over the Indian sub-continent. Cold air comes either from the north or the South and produces torrential rainfall. Some years it rains first on Sri Lanka and then travels over the Bay of Bengal. Some years it comes down from the Himalayas.

This was the month when they had decided to go back to Tarini's place. Ashok knew that they would be going most of the way by car and, if he stayed a couple of weeks, by the time he went back the weather would have settled down. He would come back the usual way, by train. So this time he decided not to take Ramu because Ashok was due to be back in Ambari in a couple of weeks' time.

So, one Saturday, Ashok, Tarini and Abhishek - now nearly a year old - packed a suitcase and sat in the car to go to Tarini's mother's house. The plan was that Tarini and Abhishek would stay there while Ashok came back to Ambari to settle and hand over the work to a newly appointed colleague. Then, whatever luggage he had, he would take along with Ramu and go down to Calcutta to the new flat he had already started renting. Then, after a couple of weeks or so, he would go back and bring Tarini and Abhishek home to Calcutta.

It was a reasonable plan and Tarini agreed. The only problem could be the weather. Sometimes in June, the monsoon could be very unpredictable. Torrential rain and lightning could arrive without warning. It all depended on the area of depression over the Indian Ocean and Bay of Bengal.

During the journey, it rained as usual and there was some waterlogging, but nothing significant. Narayan came to pick them up and everybody was delighted to see Tarini and little Abhishek. Ashok was supposed to stay for seven days but in that time, it started raining pretty heavily and there was some flooding. Over the weekend, Ashok was supposed to go back but, because of the waterlogging, Narayan said it would be impossible to drive the car. In the muddy roads the water would go into the engine.

Tarini suggested Ashok should stay for a few more days and wait for the rain to stop but Ashok said: "There is no guarantee that this rain will stop in a week or two and I have to go to hand over."

Narayan suggested he got a small dinghy to the banks of the Ganges, so that he could get the steamer to Dhaka without any trouble. Ashok had no luggage, which was helpful. So early one morning he said bye to Tarini and Abhishek and, with Narayan, sat in the dinghy. He waved to them, saying: "It's a matter of a few more days. I will come back to take you back to Calcutta."

The sky was very dark. A chill wind was blowing but it was not raining too much. Ashok said: "Let's pray it stays like that while I go to Dhaka."

After an hour or so, he arrived at the bank of the Ganges and found out that because of the rain, instead of two steamers going to Dhaka only one steamer was sailing. Ashok told Narayan to go back while he took the steamer.

He got a ticket and boarded. The steamer was very cramped. Part of the steamer had shade on the top and part was without shade. Because of the overcrowding he couldn't get a place to sit, not even a place under the shade. He thought, it's only an hour and a half before we arrive at Dhaka.

The steamer started slowly and rocked heavily from side to side. The cloud was in the corner of the sky but suddenly it came over the steamer and soon it started raining like cats and dogs.

The raindrops were as big as golf balls. Within a few minutes Ashok was completely wet. He had nothing to dry himself with. He was standing in the steamer; the rain was pouring and his skin was getting soaked. The wind was blowing very hard, driving the rain. He started feeling a bit of a chill but nothing serious.

When he got off the steamer he ran towards Dhaka rail station. He was soaked through. His hair and head were wet. He tried to buy a towel from the station but could not. People said he needed to go to the market.

He boarded the train, which was pretty empty. He found a seat, took his Punjabi off and squeezed all the water out, wiped his face and head and put on the Punjabi again. He thought when he arrived at Calcutta he would buy new clothes and change. For the time being he hoped they would dry by themselves.

The train set off and the wind coming from the window was making him shiver a bit. He started getting a headache. By the time they approached Calcutta, he was feeling quite unwell, with a headache and a dry cough. By the time they arrived he had started feeling shivery. He felt in no condition to travel on to Ambari.

By the time Ashok came off the train, he could hardly walk. He was feeling chilly and shivery. He thought it would be best if he could somehow reach Bish's studio. As he came out of the station, the sun started rising and there was a small rainbow. He went to a rickshaw and said: "Could you kindly take me to this address in Bowbazar?" The rickshaw man said: "You don't look very well. I will take you there in a few minutes. Soon they arrived outside Bish's studio.

Bishwanath was talking to Mr Shankar, the jewellery shop owner, and suddenly saw from the corner of his eye that Ashok was lying on a rickshaw seat. Immediately Bishwanath and Mr Sarkar ran towards Ashok asking what was wrong. Ashok said he was not feeling well.

Bish touched him and said: "You have got a temperature." He shouted for Manik, and they carried him to the top floor. They changed his clothes, dried him with a towel, put him to bed and covered him with as many blankets as they could.

Ashok's temperature had crept up and he started coughing non-stop. Bish said to Mr Sarkar that the wet clothes he had worn for 24 hours had given him a chest infection. He asked Ashok if he wanted to eat something but he felt a bit better lying in a bed with warm blankets.

Manik went and made some barley water. Ashok was reluctant but everybody insisted so he had some. Bish also organised some cold compress and said to Ashok: "I am sure it's nothing serious and you will get better by tomorrow." Ashok said: "I hope so."

But in the afternoon his temperature went up. Bish got a bit worried. He told Manik and Mr Sarkar to stay with Ashok and he would fetch the local doctor. In those days most of the doctors were homeopathic doctors. Although there were some licensed allopathic doctors, antibiotics had not been invented then. People had to put their faith in the homeopath.

Bish went and brought the doctor from Harrison Road. It was nearly an hour before he arrived. He felt Ashok's pulse, took his temperature and listened to his chest. He came out of the room and told Bish that Ashok had a very bad infection of the chest - air was not getting into his lungs.

The doctor said it was a very serious situation. He said he would give two medicines, but somebody had to go to his surgery for the dispensing. Bish went and got the two medicines, one syrup and two powders. The doctor asked Bish where Ashok's family was. He said if he was no better by the following day, they should let his family know he was seriously ill.

Ashok took all the medications. The three men slept on the floor to look after him through the night. In the morning, his temperature came down but the cough was persistent. Bish again went to the doctor and gave him the report. The Doctor came again in the afternoon but by the evening Ashok got worse again.

Not only did he have a temperature and cough, now he was suffering chest pain while coughing. The next morning Bish gave some money to Manik and the address of Tarini's house and said: "Go on the first train and go to her house. Be discreet, don't frighten them. But tell Narayan how serious Ashok is."

The following day Ashok's temperature remained spiky. He had not eaten for two days and his cough had become productive.

In the meantime, after a whole day's travel, Manik arrived at Tarini's house. It was not difficult to find. He was taken aback by how wealthy they were. Nobody knew Manik well but he introduced himself to Narayan and said he wanted to have a private talk with him.

When he told him how seriously ill Ashok was, Narayan couldn't believe it. He said he would go with him on the next train. He packed a bag and told Tarini what had happened to Ashok, that he had been soaked while going to Calcutta and now he had pneumonia. Narayan said he would go with Manik to Calcutta, would make sure the best doctor in Calcutta saw Ashok, and not to worry.

Manik and Narayan arrived back in Bowbazar the following morning. They ran upstairs and saw Ashok's temperature had not gone down and he had started to become delirious. Also, his limbs were very cold. Narayan tried to talk to Ashok but couldn't make out what he was saying. He was incoherent.

Narayan said to Bish: "He looks very seriously ill. Either we take him to the hospital or call one of the top doctors from there. Money should not be the issue."

From Bowbazar, two large Hospitals, Calcutta Medical and the Carmichael Hospital, were both within a couple of miles. Narayan said to Bish: "Let's go there now."

The head of the chest department was Anand Sen. He didn't do home visits but at Narayan's insistence he agreed to come and see Ashok in the flat. Overnight, Ashok's condition deteriorated. Dr Chatterjee came with his assistant and, after having a good look, he told Narayan and Bish that as well as pneumonia, Ashok now also had blood poisoning now. Mortality from there was about 50 per cent.

Ashok's breathing became very laboured. Chatterjee said: "He can be transferred to the hospital. We will start him on intravenous medicine and see how he goes."

But Ashok couldn't pull through.

The following day, he could hardly breathe. His breathing was very slow and laboured. His lips started turning blue and his condition seemed irreversible. After 10 days of struggle, and despite all the best medicines available at that time, Ashok passed away in the middle of night. He was only 33. He left behind his wife Tarini and his son, Abhishek, only one year old.

Before Ashok became very poorly, he had signed all his papers and provident fund and handed them to Narayan. Maybe in his mind he was worried he might not pull through. He told Narayan: "I have got 1,200 rupees in my provident fund and Tarini will get a pension if anything happens to me. If I don't pull through, please look after Tarini and Abhishek."

Narayan, with misty eyes, held Ashok's hands and said: "Nothing will happen to you. We are here and we will make you better. And from a money point of view, we are a big landlord and we are only one sister and three brothers. So, she will be well looked after."

Bish and Narayan were in two minds because in the Hindu religion the cremation is carried out by the son of the deceased, but Abhishek was still so small. Narayan said: "Ashok was a father figure to me, even though he was not that much older than me. I will carry out the rituals."

Bish kept saying: "Life can be so cruel. Such a young man, dying so young."

Narayan said: "I don't know what to say to Tarini. It will always haunt me whether I could have done any more."

In keeping with tradition, the body was to be cremated before sunset. Bish said: "I will go with Sarkar *Babu* and get some young men to take the body to the cremation place on the banks of the Ganges at Karatala, near Kalighat."

Bish said: "We will get a priest around there."

Narayan said: "I will give you some money to buy all the required stuff."

Bish got a new bed and a mattress on which to lay the body, which had to be cleaned and washed. He bought lots of flowers and garlands. A blanket covered the body but kept the face bare. They bought a huge amount of incense sticks and put sandal paste on his forehead.

They put the body on the bed and covered it well and four men, including Narayan and Bish, carried the body on the bed with a few young people from the locality having turned up as Bish asked them. They closed their shop and they started throwing rice (as per ritual) and chanting: "God bless and God help."

They went to the cremation place and got a priest. Narayan changed into a new *dhoti* and put on a new sacred thread, and a barber shaved his head and beard. He dipped into the Ganges and the priest started chanting and did the last ritual. Narayan had never seen a death from so near. He was nearly a broken man.

The priest was chanting: "The soul of the dead joins earth, wind, fire, water and eternal soul."

So, the ritual was done. They came out and Narayan organised a full lunch on the bank of the river for a large number of people. Narayan, with Bish and all the others, came to Bowbazar with his head shaven, barefoot, wearing a *dhoti* and a shawl. He decided to sleep on the floor for 11 days before the full *Sraddha* ritual was done. In his hands he was carrying a small blanket.

In the morning, Narayan woke up early and thanked everybody, then went to Sealdah station. It was not a religious duty for Narayan to maintain all the rituals but he decided to anyway. From the cremation, a small amount of ashes in an earthen pot had been given to Narayan. Manik packed it up well.

Narayan could now spread the ashes in the Ganges near Ashok's ancestors' home. Narayan got on the train but he couldn't sit or stand still or concentrate. His mind was all over the place. He was thinking what to say to Tarini.

Bish came to the rail station and said goodbye to Narayan. Manik also came. Narayan said to Bish: "My family will never forget what you have done for us."

Bish said: "That was nothing. The biggest tragedy was the loss of a good man."

Narayan got on to the train and fell asleep.

CHAPTER 12

Tarini was worried sick. It was six days since Narayan had gone to Calcutta and there had been no news. Anup and Akash kept saying to Tarini that no news was good news, and that the delay was because Narayan was planning to bring Ashok with him.

Narayan boarded the steamer wearing his mourning dress. The boat was full but people realised that someone near and dear to this man had passed away, so they stood up to give Narayan a seat. He thanked them, but he looked totally lost.

When the steamer arrived, everybody disembarked except him. The ferryman came and said to Narayan: "Sir, we have arrived. You need to get down."

Somehow or other, Narayan got off. There was nobody to collect him. Normally his driver came but nobody knew he was coming. It was a half-hour walk home but it took more than an hour. It was a bright, sunny day. The sun was scorching. He started sweating as he came near his house.

As he approached home he could see from afar that Tarini, with Abhishek in her lap, was standing and on either side of her were Anup and Akash. As Narayan drew nearer, it was obvious to everyone that he was wearing mourning clothes. Tarini ran to him, grabbed him and said: "What happened, Narayan?"

Narayan stood with tears pouring down his cheeks, barely able to say anything, as everyone in the house came to the porch. He simply whispered that Ashokda was no more.

Tarini fainted and fell to the floor. Her mother picked up Abhishek. Akash said: "Let's go inside." Tarini was helped to stand up and now she started crying loudly. Nobody could believe such a fit young man could die so quickly.

Narayan entered his room and, as ritual dictates, he sat on the floor and said: "Ashokda had a chest infection, then pneumonia and it caused blood poisoning. I am sorry we couldn't save him. We got the best doctor in Calcutta to treat him."

In Hindu customs, for women who lose husbands, particularly at a young age, life is full of torture. The idea is to shock the lady as much as possible so that she can recover from her loss quickly. Thank God that by this time, sati was illegal - under that practice, women were forced to die on their husband's cremation fire.

Tarini was attended to by all the ladies in the house, who were all crying. First, they cut her hair to neck length to make it less attractive. Then they took her to the house pond and all her bangles and rings were taken off. If they didn't slip off they were broken or cut off. The vermilion was wiped from her forehead. This was a custom going back centuries.

Then Tarini had to dip in the pond and clean herself. When she came out of the water, her coloured clothes were removed and replaced by a completely white sari and blouse. She came into the house with all the female members of the family as a widow, looking totally different with short hair, no *sindoor*, in all white clothes. Even Abhishek failed to recognise his mother. She was still crying inconsolably.

Narayan organised all the rituals. After 11 days the priest lit the fire and chanted all the verses. They invited about 100 people for a vegetarian meal with sweets. Tarini sat in the corner of the *pandal* with Abhishek on her lap. All the elders came and told her how sorry they were for the passing of Ashok, but also said she must be strong for Abhishek. Tarini could only look at the floor and kept crying.

A few weeks later, Narayan called Anup and Akash to his room, then asked Tarini to come in. He said he needed to discuss an important matter with everybody. Tarini was very apprehensive. Narayan said: "Ashok's death is a huge loss to all of us but the loss Tarini feels, we cannot comprehend.

"I have got two pictures of Ashok. I told Bish to frame them, one for

Tarini to keep and the other to stay on the wall in our sitting room on the wall. Tarini has got nobody from her husband's side, so I have decided to build an extension of our house especially for Tarini's requirements and for Abhishek.

"Our builder, Khan Saab, has given me a drawing and it will be two extra bedrooms with a toilet next to my room. Khan said he will take three months to complete it. So Tarini will have privacy and when Abhishek grows up, he can use the other room. We all agreed Tarini will stay with us."

Everyone agreed and then Narayan talked about money. "Ashokda died at 33 but he had a very good job and he worked for a British company. I have written to them and they will pass on his provident fund of 1,200 rupees, they will also pay three months' salary and they will give a pension in Tarini's name as his widow from the Skipton trust.

"My lawyer will bring all the papers. Tarini needs to sign so that they can release the money in Tarini's name. I suggest we get an account at the post office in Tarini's name and leave the money."

Lakshmi said: "It's a lot of money. So long Tarini gets a pension every month, she will not need any financial help as such."

Tarini cried and said: "It was very nice of you to let me know, but my world is broken. I don't need the money. You keep it, because I have to live on you people's kindness."

Narayan said: "No, Tarini, don't say that. It will be our privilege as our own older sister to keep you with us. You sign the papers and I will sort out your pension money."

PART FOUR

CHAPTER 13

Narayan's business was doing very well and Narayan himself was extremely busy but Anup and Akash were not doing very much. Slowly the rooms were built for Tarini and Abhishek. Tarini moved into her newly built rooms with Abhishek.

Time passed. Eventually, Narayan got married and both the mothers passed away. Narayan lived in the main building as *Zamindar*. His new wife was a pleasant lady called Rekha. She came from a well-off family in west Bengal called Burdwan.

Rekha was home educated but she could read and write and was very keen on reading. Narayan and his wife both stood out as a nice and decent couple. In due course they had a boy of their own. Anup and Akash started going to the office. They acted as assistants to Narayan. Slowly they got some work. Anup went to the city to buy materials and Akash started selling the crop. They also acted as Narayan's substitute when he was away.

CHAPTER 14

Abhishek started going to the village primary school, a *pathshala*. The village *pandit* and his son used to run the school for children up to 10 years old. It was outside his house in the shade of a big banyan tree. The school used to start at 10 o'clock in the morning so the boys could have a good meal before coming to school. They would study for two or three hours, then play outside in the garden, mostly football and kabaddi.

It was not advisable for Tarini, being a young widow, to go out of the house alone too often. Tarini employed a lady called Madhuri to look after Abhishek and to take him to school and bring him home. She also helped Tarini with some household chores.

Tarini would pay Madhuri from the pension money which she received every month. On a normal day, Madhuri would come between 8.30 and 9.00 am and give Abhishek a good bath after massaging him with a lot of oil, then Abhishek would have boiled rice with some boiled potatoes , some vegetables and home-made butter.

Then at 10 o'clock Abhishek would be dressed for school and, jumping up and down, would go to the *pathshala* with Madhuri. Abhishek had to carry a bag with a small blackboard, some white chalk and one or two books for his alphabets. Madhuri would come home and help Tarini and have lunch. At three o'clock she would bring Abhishek back and then go home before it was dark.

Tarini's days were not very productive. Most of the time they revolved around Abhishek. She was very good at knitting, so she had knitted jumpers for almost everyone in the family. Also, she had done some embroidery and drawings to hang on the wall.

After Abhishek went to bed, she read a book, usually by Sharad Chatterjee, by the gas lamp she had. Some days, if it was late, Madhuri would stay and sleep on the veranda. She loved Abhishek and got on very well with him. Abhishek grew up with two women in his young life, Tarini and Madhuri.

After a year or so, both Anup and Akash got married a few months apart. Now the house was full of people with Narayan's family and Anup and Akash's families. Tarini made a few friends because her sisters-in-law were her age group. She would join them for cooking some days and also for singing some songs. Things were going well. But while the other ladies could go out to the market, Tarini, as a widow, was restricted.

When Abhishek was nearly seven years old, he needed to go to a new school, a grammar school in another village. Abhishek was a bright boy. You had to take exams to get into the school and Tarini was a bit apprehensive for two reasons. First, the school was about two miles away, and second she was worried about pushing him for an exam at such a young age.

There was a small pond to cross, which in summer was not bad - but in the rainy season you had to cross a rickety bridge. Having a pond nearby meant that Abhishek was already a very good swimmer.

Tarini asked Narayan for his opinion and he said: "Abhishek has learned whatever he can from this *pathshala*. He is a bright boy. He needs more stimulation and he will be better off in a big grammar school."

But Tarini said: "In the winter months it will be dark for him to go and come back because it is an all-day school."

Narayan said: "Don't worry. I will organise a man from the firm to take him and bring him back."

Abhishek sat the exam and felt it was straightforward and simple. In due course he got a letter saying he could join the school in the new term. Abhishek was very excited because he knew this school had very good junior and senior football teams. And because this school could help him to get his matriculation.

Abhishek got new bags for the school and new clothes - a shirt and a *dhoti*. On the first day of school, Tarini gave a good puja and put a *tilak* on Abhishek. She combed his hair well, handed over his bag and gave him a two-piece coin in his pocket and said: "If you like you can buy some sweets."

One of Narayan's employees came to take him to school. Tarini stood at the door with huge apprehension about her only child's future.

The school was a big building. There were boys aged between seven and 18 in the school. So there were boys and grown-up men. The school had three big grounds and two ponds. One was for the students, who were allowed to swim as long as they knew how. There was also a ground for gymnastics. During lunch break each boy got a glass of milk and sometimes home-made cake.

Abhishek went to his class. All the boys there were new to the school. Abhishek opened his exercise book and wrote Om in Sanskrit at the top, Abhishek Banerjee below that, and so his school began.

In primary school he was taught only Bengali and Sanskrit. Now, at secondary school, he would be learning reading and writing in English. In India the custom is that when a son or daughter is about three years of age, on the day of *Saraswati Puja* their parents or an uncle teach them how to write the Sanskrit alphabet.

The custom is that you take a small, thin bamboo stick and sharpen one end like a pen. Then you dip it in a bowl of milk and, on the back of a banana leaf, your parents or your uncle hold your hand to write three alphabets. Then you give the banana leaf to the deity of Saraswati.

When Abhishek was three years old, Narayan did this ritual at home. Most of the families do their *Saraswati Puja*, the goddess of art, culture and education, at home. Narayan predicted that because he had given him *hathe khori* (his first writing), Abhishek would be very good at literature when he grew up.

Abhishek's morning timetable had changed. When he woke up he would have a fresh glass of milk and then give himself an oil massage and put some coconut oil in his black hair. Then he would jump into the pond and swim for some time before getting changed, having breakfast and doing some homework.

At about 10 o'clock he would put on his school clothes. Tarini would give him a bowl of rice with boiled potatoes, which Abhishek ate as quickly as he could. Tarini would urge him to eat slowly. He washed his hands and face and ran out of the house, saying goodbye to his mum, and started walking to school.

While walking along the road, sometimes he would have a small ball which he would kick and follow. Tarini would stand on the veranda and watch Abhishek going to school. While going to school he would meet some of his classmates on the way and have a long discussion about everything.

Abhishek was doing well in his studies and Tarini hoped and prayed that he grew up quickly and did well in school. During the day she had lots of time on her hands. She had become very friendly with Narayan's wife Rekha. Although they discussed lots of subjects, they also talked about the remarriage of widows. One of the eminent scholars of India, Vidyasagar, had started a movement to allow young widows to marry again.

Because of many pandemics a lot of young men died, leaving behind their young wives under all sorts of pressures in life, including poverty. But Tarini was very clear - she would not contemplate it. She had accepted what nature had dished out to her. She had a son and that was her life.

Tarini also felt she was lucky to have a well-off family member, her brother Narayan. That was why, whatever money she got from Ashok's employment, she handed to her brother. She had a good amount of jewellery, mainly gold, that would come in handy during Abhishek's education, and if bad times came again.

Her family had a huge amount of land but, when her father died, under British Indian law women had no right to it. So the land went to her three brothers. Although her brothers, particularly Narayan, were keen to give Tarini some land, Tarini was not interested. She was more interested in Abhishek's education.

Tarini liked reading. She bought some books from the village bookstore and during the day, while Abhishek was away, she spent her time with Rekha in the kitchen, or doing some puja, or reading the books.

She also ordered and got some full bound volumes of the epic stories *Ramayana and Mahabharata*. After lunch, sitting under the sun, she usually read one or two chapters per day. She also knitted some jumpers for Abhishek.

Abhishek had a new passion, playing football. He had recently shot up in height and he was playing with the big boys and enjoying it.

CHAPTER 15

Abhishek's schooling was going very well. He was getting good grades and came third going up to his ninth class. He was also a natural sportsman. He had become a regular player for the school football team and tended to play centre-forward. Even playing against bigger boys, he had scored some good goals. His sports teacher thought he had a good sporting career ahead of him.

During the school parents' evening, everybody's parents were coming and talking to the teachers - but nobody used to come for Abhishek. Ladies didn't come to these occasions anyway. Narayan came once or twice but Anup and Akash had no time for that sort of thing.

But one of the class teachers was very kind. Knowing that Abhishek's father had died, he used to come home and tell Tarini how Abhishek was doing , both in his studies and on the sporting field. That was a huge relief for Tarini to know.

By now everybody's children had started going to school but, for children from a wealthy *Zamindar* family, education was not the first priority. They always thought that, whether they got good or bad grades, they would end up running the family business. So it was of no consequence what grades they got.

Narayan's business was doing well. He had expanded it recently. Anup and Akash seemed to spend more time pigeon shooting and had the latest guns. Now they took up other hobbies like fishing and horse riding. At times they did help in the business, but most of the time they were missing. Narayan didn't mind that; without them, he seemed to function better.

Tarini, on the other hand, spent every minute and second thinking about Abhishek. Many of the family members thought that she was spoiling the boy a bit. Now the family had expanded for everybody and Narayan had decided who had which room. Until now Tarini had been sleeping in a bed, while Abhishek used to sleep on a low platform in the same room.

But now Tarini got a room of her own – a large room with a few *almirahs* holding her all-white clothes. Abhishek got a smaller room with a study attached to it, with a table and chair and a mirror.

Tarini now got up at the crack of dawn and would get ready and changed and go to the puja room. As a widow she was not supposed to touch anything there, so Tarini would sit and read the *Gita*, which gave her some peace of mind. Then she would go to Abhishek's room and wake him up, which was a difficult job. Then she gave breakfast to Abhishek.

Every morning Narayan asked Tarini how Abhishek was doing and. When he bumped into Abhishek he would ask how his football was going and tell him that if he gave a couple of weeks' notice Narayan would make sure he came to watch him. Everybody in the family knew that Narayan had a soft spot for Abhishek.

Now in the house there were lots of people to feed including lots of maids, so after breakfast the ladies sat down and decided what to make for lunch and dinner. Tarini just sat and listened but didn't get involved or engaged in the discussion.

After coming home from school, Abhishek would have another shower and then sit down to study. He was told that he should read aloud so that he could hear himself. Then he would do some Maths. The difficulty was that nobody in the house could help him with his homework.

Then every evening he had to memorise a poem in English because at school his class teacher would call students randomly and ask them to recite poetry from memory. If you did well, you would be praised - but if you didn't, you would have to stand outside the class. So Abhishek was very serious before going to bed and would study for at least two hours.

Some mornings Tarini had to shout to wake Abhishek up because he was so tired from playing football that he needed to sleep longer. Football was bare-footed in those days and Abhishek would have his own clothes for playing football, where he had started scoring goals.

School was going well. He was not very good at music but he had taken part in some of the school debates and had been class monitor. This meant he had to control the boys in his class and the juniors as well. And he was very popular.

Last year he had come third in his class exams and his school report was good, but he was working hard so that he could be second or first this time. Normal school finished at four o'clock but he would play five-a-side football and by the time he went home it could be very dark. From a distance he could see a lady standing with a kerosene lamp. He knew it was his mother. Abhishek used to tell her not to wait outside for him but Tarini would not listen.

By now Narayan, Anup and Akash were all married and had small children. But Abhishek was the oldest child in the house. He was selected for the junior district football team and he played well. He was given the centre-forward role, so he scored some goals.

But Anup and Akash kept telling him that playing football wouldn't give him a living and he needed to concentrate on his studies more. Abhishek used to listen to them without answering back.

Over the next year Abhishek became much taller. He was a big lad now and he was playing in the Dhaka league, but Tarini was very worried that he might do badly in his exams. Also, he mixed with a lot of people from different places and the situation in the country was volatile because of the Quit India movement.

The racial tension over the possible division of the country was pretty high. The Congress party was led by Mohandas Gandhi and, although he was talking about non-violence, some of the party were committing violence underground.

There was a big faction of the Muslim League, led by Muhammad Jinna, that was clear in its desire to have a Muslim state, which would mean dividing the country in two. Abhishek kept reassuring his mother that he was not in any trouble but he was in senior school and a lot of boys there were members of Subash Bose's Forward Bloc party. They wanted to fight it out with the English rulers.

Abhishek went to the gym to build his muscles for sport, but people said some of the revolutionaries were permanent fixtures there. These gyms used to have a lot of weight-lifting facilities and there was wrestling. Abhishek took part in some of the wrestling for fun.

He knew a lot of the revolutionaries but his focus was different. He wanted to get his matriculation, get a job in Calcutta and take his mother with him. Tarini was looked after very well, but Abhishek knew that for a young widow, living in her brother's house was not the best thing.

There was a final year student from the same village called Alok, who was one of the leaders of the underground movement. Abhishek knew him but was not very friendly with him. One day outside the gym, Alok gave Abhishek a big, bound book and said: "Could you keep it safe in your house for a couple of weeks?"

Abhishek asked: "What is special about the book that you can't keep in your own house?"

Alok said: "Open the book, you will know."

Abhishek opened the book and there was a handgun fitted inside it. Abhishek said: "Why are you giving it to me?"

Alok said: "I used this gun in a Dhaka procession last week, so the police are after me. Why you? Because you have a big house and your uncle is a very good pal of a police officer. They won't have any suspicion."

Abhishek was still very reluctant but two other boys came over and said: "Keep it for a few days and don't worry. We will take it back from you."

Abhishek took it reluctantly, put it in the bag, then hurriedly went home and put the book under his bed. Nobody knew anything.

About two weeks later, Abhishek was in a history lesson when, through the window, he saw a police jeep entering the school. The police officer went to the office of the head teacher, Bijen *Babu,* and said: "Sir, you are harbouring terrorism in the school."

Bijen *Babu* said: "I don't understand what you are talking about. Can you explain?"

The police officer sat down and said: "You have got a student called Alok Das. We have arrested him for shooting a gun in Dhaka city and he is in our custody. He is the boy who caused another bombing in another town about a month ago. He is working for the Quit India Movement.

Bijen *Babu* said: "He is only 18 years old."

The policeman said: "He had a mask on but through a tip-off we arrested him. After a bit of a beating he has confessed - and he has also confessed that he has given the gun to Abhishek Banerjee for safe keeping."

Bijen *Babu* said: "I think you got it wrong. Abhishek is a very decent and bright boy."

The police officer said: "As he is a minor, I want to question him in front of you."

Bijen *Babu* said: "Fine. You have a cup of tea."

Instead of calling a *peon,* Bijen *Babu* went to fetch Abhishek himself. Bijen *Babu* realised the gravity of the matter and went to the history class. Seeing the head teacher, everybody stood up.

Bijen *Babu* said: "Abhishek, can you come with me?" Then he told the teacher to continue with the class. Bijen *Babu* took Abhishek to the back of the school and said: "Tell me the truth. Did Alok give you a gun?"

Abhishek fumbled and said: "Yes, he gave me a book to keep for two weeks."

Bijen *Babu* said: "The police are here for that. Tell me, where is the gun?"

Abhishek said: "It's in my bedroom."

Bijen *Babu* said: "Listen very carefully. There is a big wall at the back of the school. Can you climb it? Take your school bag, climb over the wall and, using the back road, go home. Take the book out and go to the nearest part of the Ganges and throw it in a deep part of the river. I will deal with the police."

Abhishek did exactly what the head teacher said. It was difficult to climb the wall but he managed it, then ran as fast as he could towards home.

Bijen *Babu* came running to his office perspiring profusely and drying his forehead with his handkerchief. He said to the police officer: "I am sorry for being late. I am sorry, I was looking for Abhishek everywhere in the school but couldn't find him. I am not sure whether he has been to school today but if you leave it to me, I will talk to Abhishek tomorrow. I am sure there is a misunderstanding."

The police officer finished his tea and said: "Don't worry, Bijen *Babu*. Abhishek comes from a very good family. His uncle, Mr Narayan Mukherjee, is a very respectable man. I know him well. While going back, I will talk to him so he makes sure Abhishek stays out of this Quit India movement."

Meanwhile, Abhishek arrived home huffing and puffing. He said: "I need to take something from my room and give it to a friend and I will be back soon."

He took the book in his bag, ran as fast as he could and waited for the darkness to descend a bit, then threw the book as far as he could into the Ganges. He immediately felt a sense of relief and slowly started walking home.

When he arrived home a bit late, the house was like a ghost house. Everybody seemed to be very quiet. Tarini looked as if she had been crying all afternoon, her eyes were swollen. Abhishek went to his room but Tarini came and said: "Come with me, your uncle wants to talk to you."

Abhishek said: "What about?"

Tarini said: "Come now, you will know."

The Mukherjees' sitting room was a large one. There were lots of chairs and stools. When Tarini and Abhishek came to the room, everyone was sitting. Narayan and his wife, Anup and Akash and their wives were already there and Tarini went to sit in the corner. Abhishek stayed standing.

Narayan said: "What we are going to discuss has to stay in this room. A police officer came to my office to see me. According to them, Abhishek was involved with a bombing and shooting in Dhaka city on behalf of the Quit India movement. And Abhishek possesses a gun."

Abhishek fumbled and said: "That is not true."

Akash said: "Just shut up and listen."

Narayan continued: "The police will not take any action this time because you are my nephew, but they will not tolerate any breach in future."

By now Tarini was crying pretty loudly. But Narayan said: "I made it a point to go to your school and speak to your head teacher. I am happy to forgive you this time because your head teacher spoke so highly about you."

Then Narayan raised his voice and said: "A gun was brought into my house! Look, we know you haven't got your father. But we all try our best to make you a decent man and now it seems you are going out of hand and we are failing you. Where is the gun now?"

Abhishek said: "As Bijen *Babu* advised, I have thrown it in the Ganges."

Akash said: "How do we believe you?"

Narayan said: "You are telling me there is no gun in the house?"

Abhishek said: "That is correct."

Anup said to Narayan: "This boy is in bad company. He is not going to study. Let him start working and earning a living for himself."

Akash said: "He makes a very good cup of tea. Why don't you make a tea stall for him in the city? He will run it well."

Tarini dried her eyes and said: "Please give him another chance . I promise it won't happen again."

Narayan was the man who made all the decisions in the house. He said: "Abhishek, do you want to say anything?"

"No," said Abhishek, his head bowed. "It won't happen again."

Narayan said: "I am very impressed by what your head teacher said, so we will give you a chance."

To lighten the mood slightly, he added: "Your teacher says you are a very good centre-forward so, whenever the next match is, you let me know and I will watch it."

Recently Abhishek had built up a lot of muscle going to the gym. Being more than six feet tall, with broad shoulders and thick, dark hair, he stood out as a very handsome man. He also got a lot of invitations to play football in many tournaments. Narayan kept his promise and came to watch Abhishek play.

This year was his matriculation year and he was revising as hard as he could, while Tarini was busy doing pujas to every deity for his exam success. Because he was taking the English Board exam, the test centre was in Dhaka. A transport was organised to take him for his exams - but football got in the way.

He did fairly well in the exams but would have got a better grade had he concentrated slightly harder. The question arose as to what to do next.

Narayan suggested that he get admitted to Dhaka University, stayed in the campus and travelled on weekends to see his mother. But Abhishek in his mind had decided to start a job first and study later. Tarini was suggesting otherwise but Abhishek said privately to her: "I am going to Calcutta and as soon as I get a job, you will come with me."

After a week he travelled to Calcutta, upsetting most of his family members. Somebody got him the address of a bedsit, and also the address of an important man from the village who was settled in Calcutta, called Neeluda. Whoever travelled from the village and the area around it used to land up with Neeluda, and so did Abhishek.

Neeluda took him to the coffee house near Calcutta University, opposite Presidency College. This place had an intellectual flavour. It was where all the revolutionary, intellectual young people used to come for a good chat and coffee. Abhishek met a large number of young men and a few women there. Neeluda introduced him as the footballer who came out of the village.

Everybody said the job market was very flat because of the political uncertainty and recurrent riots. Abhishek was getting very frustrated when a young, enthusiastic guy called Ashish said to Abhishek: "I hear you are a good footballer, which position do you play?"

Abhishek said: "Centre-forward."

Ashish said: "Why don't you have a trial for our company team? Our company, Wimco, is a new British company outside Calcutta. We manufacture matchboxes and we have got a good football team - they are trialling for a few players this Saturday."

Abhishek said: "Can you organise a trial for me?"

Ashish said: "That's not a problem."

Abhishek's money was running out, so he was happy. Ashish took him on the Saturday to the Wimco factory. It was a shining, newly built factory with a large football ground in the middle of it. Ashish gave him a form. He filled it in and realised there were six places available - and 50 people had turned up already.

A gentleman called Frank was in charge and he had many assistants with him, so he divided the 50 players into 10 teams, each playing half an hour against each other. It went on from morning to afternoon. Then Frank specifically asked Abhishek to take some penalties. Abhishek scored four out of five.

In the evening, Frank assembled everybody. From a piece of paper he read out five names - those who had been successful. Abhishek's trial had gone well but the competition was fierce, so he was pleased and surprised that he had been selected as centre-forward for the Wimco team.

He asked Frank what he needed to do and Frank said: "Go home. You will get a letter of appointment within a week."

Abhishek asked: "What will be the job?"

Frank said: "To score goals. We are in the Calcutta League and we want to do well this year, so your job will be practising Monday to Friday and playing on Saturday. Of course, don't forget to sign the papers of the company - otherwise you won't get paid."

Abhishek was delighted but the next thing to arrange was somewhere to stay. The factory was outside Calcutta, near Dunlop Bridge, but on match days the players were taken by the company bus from the factory to the ground and back. He thought if he got a rented property near the factory, he could cycle there and go to matches in the bus.

One of his factory colleagues told him: "About two miles away, there is a place called Belgharia, where they have built quite a few flats and terraced houses."

Abhishek went to see a rental property which had one big bedroom, a small sitting room, a kitchen-cum-dining room and an outside toilet. The rent was 11 rupees per month. But the owner, Mr Roy, said: "I only rent to married people."

Abhishek said: "It's for me and my mother, because my mother is a widow. She will stay with me."

Mr Roy said: "In that case, that's fine. I will send a cleaner to clean the house. Where is your luggage?"

Abhishek said: "I have none, but I will slowly buy."

"Where is your mother going to sleep?"

"To start with, maybe on the floor."

"Don't worry," said Mr Roy. "I will send a bed for your mother."

Abhishek paid an advance and said they would move in by the end of the month. He would put a sofa-cum-bed in the sitting room for him to sleep on. He had a month before starting the new job, so he took the key of the house and decided to buy few things before going to the village to bring Tarini.

The next week Abhishek arrived at the Mukherjees' house with a big smile on his face and told Tarini: "I have got a job, pack up your clothes. We are leaving."

Tarini was very hesitant about what the family members would think but, in her heart, she was very proud that Abhishek had got a job and a rented house. That evening, at the dining table, with all his uncles and aunts there, Abhishek said: "I need to tell you something. I have got a job for the big British company Wimco in Calcutta."

Everybody congratulated him and Narayan asked: "What is the job?"

Abhishek said: "Centre-forward for the Wimco company football team."

Akash said: "So it's not a proper job then."

Abhishek said: "Whatever it is, it's a job. I have got a rented house in Belgharia and I have already got furniture and utensils, so I want to take my mother with me next week."

Narayan angrily stood up and said: "What's the rush? You just got a job, settle there and take your time. Nobody will stop you from taking your mother."

Anup said: "Who will be doing the cooking and cleaning? Your mother is not used to that."

Akash said: "Don't try to show off. These footballing jobs are very fickle. If you can't score, they will sack you."

All three of them told him to go and start his job but to leave Tarini alone. Once he settled, he could come back for her. Abhishek decided not to argue but as he went to his room he told Tarini: "I don't want to keep you here for a single extra day."

Tarini said: "Leave it to me. I will talk to Narayan again."

The next day, Tarini went to talk to her brothers, saying: "Abhishek is very upset. He doesn't want to disobey any of you but he wants to take me when he starts his job and moves into his house."

Narayan called Abhishek and said: "I understand you are so keen to take your mother with you. So keep this 200 rupees and take your mother. Make sure you get someone to help her."

Abhishek said: "Uncle, at the end of the month I will get a salary."

Anup said: "Don't argue. Just listen when your elders tell you something."

Akash said: "Your mother is not used to hardship. If there is any problem at any stage, let us know and we will bring *Didi* back."

Seven days later, the car was packed for Tarini and Abhishek's move. Narayan came outside and Abhishek touched his feet. Narayan said to Tarini: "I have got some money from your account. If you want, you could take it because you may need it."

Tarini said: "The money is safe with you. If I need it, I will ask."

After 24 hours' travel, Tarini and Abhishek arrived at their new home. Tarini was delighted that at least Abhishek had his own place. But it was a bit hard to move from such a big house to a one-bedroom terraced house.

Within two minutes, Tarini gave a big list to Abhishek of things to buy from the market. Mr Roy came and said he had already furnished the house with things from his own home.

He greeted Tarini and said: "If there is anything I can do to help, please give me a shout. I don't live very far away."

CHAPTER 16

Abhishek started his job. He was woken up at six o'clock by his alarm clock, had some breakfast and cycled to the Wimco factory. It took about 45 minutes and when he arrived he changed and went to the ground, where practice started.

Frank was in charge. He made them run four times around the ground, then they got a fruit juice and some nuts and then the football practice started. Frank, with a whistle, kept shouting.

At midday, when the sun became very hot, the players would come to the gym, have a quick shower, change and have a free lunch at the factory canteen. At about one o'clock an officer came with a time sheet – and that was your day's work done. So the players were looked after very well.

This went on from Monday to Thursday. Friday was a day off. On Saturday, Abhishek would come to the company for match day, either a home or away fixture.

Abhishek played well and scored a few goals. The company management was happy with the team. A large number of people watched the matches, so Abhishek was now a well-known face in the sporting circle. Tarini was stuck in a small room but she was very happy. It was her son's house and he was doing well.

One day, Abhishek said to Tarini: "Do you remember Himanshu from our class?"

"Why?"

"He came to see me to play football. He told me he is not getting a job and he has nowhere to stay. He asked me if he could stay with us for some time."

Tarini said: "That's fine, but where is he going to sleep?"

Abhishek said: "The kitchen floor. When you finish your cooking, we could put a mattress down."

From the following week there were three people in the house. Himanshu, a jovial guy, was very grateful to Abhishek. He said to Tarini: "Thanks for saving me. I cannot go back to the village. I need to have a job. Now that Abhishek is a football star, I am sure he will be able to sort out a job for me."

After a lot of pestering by Tarini, Abhishek got himself admitted to a BSc course at Calcutta University, an evening course. After practice he could take a bus and go to College Square. It wasn't every night and Abhishek thought it would be useful once he finished his football career.

The season went very well. The Managing Director of the company, Mr Miller, came to watch a few matches and was very impressed with Abhishek. At the end-of-year dinner, Abhishek took Himanshu along and introduced him to Mr Miller.

Mr Miller said: "Yes, I have seen this guy. He carries your bag."

Abhishek said: "He is a classmate from my village and he is looking for a job."

Mr Miller said: "Wimco is full, we have no jobs. But our sister company is expanding. They make bricks in the quarry. It's a very hard job. But if you want, I could give him a job there."

Himanshu was delighted. Tarini cooked a big dinner for all of them. Abhishek and Tarini went to the village for a couple of weeks and Tarini was nicely surprised that lot of people at the rail station had seen Abhishek's picture and knew him as a footballer.

Narayan looked much older nowadays. He was very tense because he sent most of his products to Calcutta and, with fighting breaking out and more rumours about the division of the state, the situation had become very stressful. Many of the Hindu landlords had sold their property and moved over to West Bengal.

Abhishek and Tarini, after two breaks, came back to Belgharia again. Now the close-season practice started again - for Abhishek, life was moving on at a good pace.

There was a footballing scout who came and asked to speak privately with Abhishek. He took him to a corner and said: "The Lever Company is an international company that makes mustard oil, coconut oil and a variety of soaps and cleansing substances. They have opened a new factory but their football team is not doing very well. This is just an informal enquiry; if they doubled your salary, would you be interested in joining them?"

Abhishek was in two minds. By now he had spent one-and-a-half years at Calcutta University. He sounded out Mr Roy, who said: "Take it. You don't get this sort of offer every day."

Abhishek said: "In that case, I need a two-bedroom house - a bedroom for me and one for my mother."

By now Mr Roy had grown fond of Abhishek, so he organised a two-bedroom terraced house with a kitchen and a bathroom.

Himanshu had his own place but he turned up every Saturday to watch football and every Sunday to have Tarini's cooked lunch.

Abhishek enjoyed playing for Lever this season. The facilities were good and they were third in the league. In the last game of the year, Abhishek was dribbling the ball near the penalty box when the opposition centre-back kicked his calf. Abhishek fell to the ground in excruciating pain.

He was carried off on a stretcher and taken to Calcutta Medical College. A ruptured Achilles tendon was diagnosed and he was put in a long plaster cast and given crutches. There would be no more football for a while. The plaster was changed after six weeks for a smaller one that he wore for three weeks, then he had extensive physio treatment.

Abhishek started walking again, but it took him nearly six months to get over the limping. He did manage to practise but he had lost his speed and some of the power of his kicking. He realised he might not be able to play football at a high level again.

He considered going into the management of sports. Lever also had a good cricket team and Abhishek was invited to join it as a player. He had played cricket in the past but this time he found he could score a few runs and could bowl off-spin.

By now, as a sportsman and as a graduate, Abhishek knew he should be able to get a decent job. He realised his sporting career might not go on for long. The options were to go into sports management or a corporate managerial job, keeping sports as a hobby.

He had a few interviews but getting a promotion was difficult. Abhishek decided to hold on to his current job as a night shift assistant manager for the time being and get some more experience in management. His only worry was that Tarini had to stay alone at night. Tarini had asked Mr Roy to look for a suitable girl for Abhishek and Mr Roy did try, but people were not interested in a chap who played football for a soap company.

Time passed smoothly and one day one of the matchmakers said to Tarini: "There is a very good-looking girl, you could see her for Abhishek. She has studied up to ninth class and her father was a General Practitioner in Dhaka. But due to the recent riot they have become refugees and he now lives in a rented house.

"But I bet my bottom dollar that you will like the girl. She is a very sweet-looking girl."

CHAPTER 17

Vivek Ganguly was a well-established General Practitioner in Dhaka. His practice was not very far from the river Ganges. He had two chambers on both sides of the river and he also dispensed medicines from both of them. He had two full-time compounders and two full-time *peons*-cum-receptionists in the surgery.

His family were well-established people from the city of Dhaka, so it was no wonder that he went to a local school and the local university. While still attached to his hospital job, he got married to a rich land-owner's daughter called Rani, whose family came from a place called Burdwan in the west of Bengal.

Being the only daughter, she had a large amount of gold and cash. So Vivek decided to start his own practice, with one chamber in the posh area of Dhaka and another in a slightly poorer part of the city.

Because there were few doctors around, his practice picked up very quickly and he became a successful GP with a thriving practice. He bought some land a few years after starting his practice and, with an architect, built a house. It was a relatively good-sized house with a statue of the deities Laxmi and Ganesh at the entrance. He had a car and a driver.

His two compounders-cum-assistants were Kalim and Ashghar. They were like family members and they used to live not very far from Vivek's house. After a few years, Vivek and Rani had three daughters and a son. His life was very busy but smooth and pleasant. He managed to get his eldest daughter married pretty young to a businessman from Calcutta.

But the atmosphere in Dhaka became very toxic. The religious tension was out of control. All this nonsense had got out of hand and every day there were stories of arson, violence, rape and murder.

Vivek was mostly concerned that, during most of the day and night, he was not at home. Rani was alone with two young girls and a young boy. Although there were maids and servants in the house, Rani didn't feel very safe.

One day Vivek, while coming back from the rough part of Dhaka, was attacked by a mob. Although he didn't feel it was racial, he could not rule it out. He was very shaken. Rani kept telling him that it was high time that they left and went to Calcutta.

Vivek asked: "Doing what? How can we go, leaving everything here?"

But a few days later a young Hindu girl was kidnapped, raped and murdered. Nobody knew who did it, but it brought home the reality of the situation. Vivek spoke to Ashghar and Kalim, who both suggested that, while the tension was at its height, he would be better off going to Calcutta and coming back when things had settled down. They decided enough was enough.

Kalim said to Vivek: "Sir, you cannot go to Calcutta on the normal route because there are many pockets of rioting on the way. It is not safe. I have planned out a different route that, although longer, will be safer. As safe as it can be under the circumstances.

Vivek said in a tense voice: "Sit down and tell me - what's your plan?"

Kalim said: "I will drive you all as far as I can go towards West Bengal. Then my friend Javed will take you in a boat and he will also go as far as it is safe for him to go. This will be to the Hoogly River. At this point you have to find another boat on your own. I'm sure you will be fine. It should not be a problem as there are plenty of boats going up and down.

"This is the safest plan in my opinion. God willing, things will settle down soon and you will be able to come back soon. Trust me, I will look after everything here."

So, soon after this conversation, Vivek asked them to pack up all the bags. Rani told her two daughters and son and they got three big suitcases and packed all their gold and jewellery. Vivek did not want to leave his birthplace but he thought it was best for his daughters.

Kalim had been working for nearly 20 years with Vivek. He said he would look after his house and property. As discussed, Javed *Bhai* had a long boat. He came to Vivek's house and repeated his concerns that Vivek and Kalim had discussed previously: "I can take you in the middle of the night in my boat, but I will take you only to a place outside Calcutta. After that you have to find your way, because Hindus are killing Muslims in Howrah. I cannot go that far."

One dark new-moon night, they all very quietly got into their car, kept the headlights off and put a blanket over the girls. Kalim drove the car towards the Ganges. On the road, a group of young people stopped his car. Kalim put the window down and said: "Salaam Alaikum. We are going to the other side of town to see our relatives."

One young man shouted: "Let them go, they are one of us."

They reached the quiet part of the Ganges, where Javed was waiting with his boat. In the dark night, without making any noise, Vivek, Rani and their two daughters and the sleeping son got on the boat. Javed put a blanket over the children.

Kalim put all the bags in the boat and, crying, said: "I will look after everything here. *Babu*, you don't worry. You have been very good to us. God will be kind to you, *Inshallah*," Then he left.

Javed and his son started rowing the boat as quietly as they could. He told everybody to keep their heads down. When they passed through the main port, there were a few men standing with swords in their hands. Javed stood up and said: "Brothers, salaam. We are going to the new town, not very far."

The guy said: "Why in the night?"

Javed answered: "One of our relatives is poorly."

So they let him go. Vivek thought it was the narrowest escape they had had. After several hours in the boat in the dark, slowly the sun rose in the east. The Ganges looked very calm. There was only the fluttering noise of the water.

Javed whispered: "*Sahib*, we are in Sonarghat. We will not go any further and it's morning now. In a few hours you will get transport here, a taxi. Let me go."

In the dark, Vivek took all the luggage, his two daughters and his sleeping son off the boat. Rani sat on the grass verge of the Ganges. Javed said: "Good luck to you, sir."

He had already been paid a large amount of money but Vivek hugged him and said: "Javed *Bhai*, thanks for saving our life." He had a gold bangle in his hand and he gave it to Javed and said: "A small token for your hard work."

Javed touched Vivek's feet and said: "When this madness stops soon, we will see you again." He wiped his face and eyes with a scarf and took the boat back towards Dhaka.

Rani was sitting on the grass, holding the children. There was one blanket for three of them. The cold breeze was not helping. It was nearly dawn but Vivek was very impatient as the sun rose slowly. He paced on the banks of the river and wondered what fate held for him and his family.

Vivek did some calculations and realised he was about eight miles away from Calcutta. He thought it might be better to take another boat to Calcutta dock. He had plenty of cash with him.

At about six o'clock all the boats started to come in. One guy agreed to take them to Calcutta port and he also agreed to take them to Kali Ghat, where Vivek wanted to go. But he would charge double. The boatman asked his name and Vivek, by now a bit agitated, said: "What for?"

The guy said: "I want to know whether you are Hindu or not."

"Yes."

"In that case I can take you because the bridge near the Howrah is not safe for Muslims. There is a lot of killing going on."

Vivek wanted to go to Kalighat because it was situated on the banks of the Ganges and one of his nephews had a flat there. He had the address on a small piece of paper.

After an hour or so, the small boat arrived at the banks of Kalighat. The boatman, called Gouranga, was very kind: He asked Vivek: "It seems you are very stressed. How can I help you?"

Vivek said: "Can you take all the luggage and my family and sit on the bank of the river while I go and fetch my nephew?"

Gouranga said: "How long will you take?"

Vivek said: "I am not sure but I will come back as soon as possible."

Gouranga said: "That will ruin my day's business, but under the circumstances I will hang around."

Vivek started running. He knew Jagdish, his nephew, lived near to the town centre and he also heard he lived on a corner. By now Vivek was very stressed and dishevelled but, after asking lots of random people, eventually he found the flat.

When he knocked on the door, it was opened and Jagdish was standing there, completely taken aback to see Vivek.

Vivek told him to come quickly, so they ran to the boat and found out everybody sitting there, not having eaten or drunk for nearly 24 hours. Gouranga helped them to take all the luggage and they reached Jagdish's flat.

Vivek was worried about the flat. He had got the impression from Jagdish that he had a large place but it was only a one-bedroom flat, very cramped with a toilet downstairs. Vivek thought they had better stay in this place that night but, he told Rani, he would find a better place tomorrow.

Jagdish helped to get some food, which everyone enjoyed. He worked for a drama company. In those days his salary was pretty poor and sometimes payment was ad-hoc. No work, no pay. Jagdish said he would stay with a friend if Vivek needed to stay for longer. Vivek was not used to living like this but the truth came to him that he was now nothing but a refugee.

Vivek was not worried about money. At least he had brought plenty of cash and jewellery. The following day, with Jagdish's help, he found a three-bedroom flat near the Kali temple. It was just a ground floor flat. But the toilet was inside the house and there was an abundant water supply from the Calcutta Corporation.

The landlord was a bit greedy. Realising Vivek's predicament, he wanted a large amount in advance. Vivek had no choice because he didn't know anybody here, so he obliged.

The following day, the house was clean. The children were pleased to have a decent flat. Jagdish's friend helped to transfer the luggage and now Vivek had an address: 7 Kalighat Road, Calcutta 10.

Vivek told Rani she had to spend money wisely unless Vivek got a job - they had two daughters to get married. From a rich man's food habit, they started eating very bland, cheap food. He also decided that his two daughters should stay at home and get educated there, though he sent his son to a local school.

The daughters were keen to go to school but Vivek told them that financially, and because they were in a rough place, it was best to study at home. He would buy all the books.

Vivek knew in his heart that going back to Dhaka would not happen. After what he had seen while coming to Calcutta, there was no way he would put his family through the same risks. He thought about starting a new practice but realised that to start an establishment would cost a lot of money. He didn't know what to do.

His routine was very mundane. He would have a cup of tea and then go to the local market, buy some vegetables and fish, read the newspaper, have lunch, and walk for a mile or two. In the evening he would go to the local park, sit on a bench and contemplate life.

But he made some new friends in the park. He talked to them about politics, mainly independence and the division of Bengal, and would then come home and have dinner. In those days there was no television, so he listened to the radio before going to bed.

From having a hectic life, his lifestyle had become very dull. It bothered Vivek many times and he would get depressed, but at his stage of life there was very little he could do to change things.

CHAPTER 18

Abhishek was an assistant manager with a good salary and Tarini had converted their house into a lovely home. She wrote letters, particularly to Narayan and Rekha. They promised to come and visit.

Abhishek's company cricket team played in the league. He had become a regular batsman and he had enough time to practise. He scored a century against Calcutta's Gymkhana club.

The English clubs in Calcutta had started a league and were looking for an honorary secretary. Ever since Abhishek ruptured his Achilles tendon, he knew his sporting career would finish very soon, but he wanted to continue in the sporting field.

He applied for the secretary position for the Calcutta league and was the best candidate for the job, so he got it. One of his friends who had a printing press printed cards for him: Abhishek Banerjee, BSc, Assistant Manager Lever Company, Honorary Secretary Calcutta Cricket League. Abhishek bought a lot of new clothes for his multiple activities. He had also become a very good speaker.

Abhishek applied for a few more jobs but everybody wanted experience, which he didn't have. So he decided to stay with the Lever company. During this time, one lady friend of Tarini told her that she saw a very good-looking girl in the *Durga Puja pandal* and she immediately thought about Abhishek.

She said: "I know the family. They recently came from outside Dhaka. I understand they were reasonably well-off but they are now refugees - they are staying in a rented house in Kalighat. If you like, I could organise for Abhi to see the girl."

But Tarini said Abhishek was extremely busy with his job and cricket. It would be better if she went with Himanshu and saw the girl. When Himanshu heard that, he said: "No worries. I know what Abhishek will like."

Abhi also said that although uncle Bishwanath was his father's friend, it would be good to take him. Tarini said: "No, I am not coming. You have to go. Although Bishwanath is a bit old now and his son runs the business, if we ask I am sure he will come."

One Saturday afternoon, Abhishek, Himanshu and Bishwanath went to Mr Ganguly's house to see Sharmila. They were given lots of food and sweets to make them happy, then Sharmila came out with her mother.

Although Abhishek kept looking at the floor, he could tell she was very good looking, a real beauty. After a few minutes, Bishwanath said: "Sharmila can go, we don't want to embarrass her too long." Abhishek felt more comfortable.

There was silence for a few minutes, then Vivek said: "I should make one point very clear. I was a relatively well-established man but unfortunately, for my daughters' sake I left everything behind. Basically, I am living a refugee's life. I will not be able to give anything as a gift or dowry. I thought, before things go further, I should make this point very clear."

Bishwanath said: "I am glad you raised this point. The Banerjee family is against dowry and has raised a lot of petitions to remove the custom from marriage.

"I am not related to them, but I know the family very well. They only want your daughter. I knew Abhishek's father very well. He was one of the most decent men I have come across. His son will be an excellent husband and will look after your daughter."

They suggested that after speaking to Tarini they would confirm. But Bish said in Vivek's ear: "I think we will go ahead."

When they came out of Kalighat, at the rail station Abhishek and Himanshu had a row. Himanshu said: "What was the point for you to come if you decided to look at the floor for an hour?"

Now Abhishek, through his job and sporting activities, had a lot of good contacts. Through one of his sporting friends, he came to know that the Indian Chemical company was building a new factory and was advertising for a manager's post.

Indian Chemical was expanding throughout the country. It made all sorts of oil and chemical products and household goods. He applied and did a lot of preparation for the interview. In the meantime, Tarini went to her village to see her brothers and sisters-in-law.

Business was expanding in India, with many new factories and offices opening up. Meanwhile, the Quit India movement was also gaining a lot of momentum. Unfortunately, there seemed to be a religious riot almost every month.

Abhishek went for the interview. It was a tough one but by the end the English Chief Executive thought that Abhishek was a very dynamic young man - so he was offered the job, with an excellent salary and perks. The factory was outside Calcutta in a place called Kamarhati, but the head office was in Esplanade, in the heart of the city. Abhishek would be in the office for three days each week and in the factory for two.

At this stage, Kamarhati was still full of jungle, so they were cutting it back and building the plant and houses for the workers. The company also offered a newly built house with six bedrooms, and a driver and car.

Tarini was delighted with Abhishek's career and she suggested that before joining the new job he should get married. Abhishek said to his mother: "I don't want to put a lot of pressure on Mr Ganguly. It will be a simple marriage in his place, but I will throw a party in one of Calcutta's top hotels."

Tarini, Vivek and a priest went through the Holy Book - Tarini was very superstitious - and they fixed a date for the marriage. Abhishek, through one of his printing friends, produced 100 cards in English and 100 in Bengali saying: "Mrs Sharmila and Abhishek Banerjee invite you to their marriage celebration in the Grand Hotel in Calcutta." He had to do an English one because most of his company executives and cricket friends were English.

Mr Ganguly made a small *pandal* outside his house in Kalighat. Abhishek and his few friends, Himanshu and Bishwanath and his family, went to the marriage and, in accordance with the Hindu custom, got married.

The weekend after the marriage was Abhishek's party in the Grand Hotel. It went on from evening to early morning. The musicians played lots of music and all his friends danced and enjoyed themselves.

After the marriage they came back to their flat and started their family life. Sharmila began to like her mother-in-law. Tarini had never had a daughter, so they quickly bonded like mother and daughter. Tarini would encourage Sharmila to cook different things on different days and also encouraged Abhishek to take his new wife to the theatre and cinema.

After a month of marriage, the happy couple went back to the Gangulys' for a weekend. Abhishek could make out that they were in a bit of financial difficulty. He went and bought as much as he could from the shops and he came to know that Chandan, Sharmila's young brother, had been sent home from school for not paying fees for three months.

Abhishek decided to stay until the Monday and went to speak to the headmaster. He settled all the fees and told the headteacher that from now on he would be paying them. The headmaster wouldn't need to write letters to Mr Ganguly.

Before they left, Mr Ganguly also informed Abhishek that, while was very reluctant to discuss it, his younger daughter had got a good proposal from a decent chap who worked in an insurance company. Abhishek said: "What's the problem?"

Vivek said hesitantly: "It's not the boy, but the family wants a substantial dowry and it is not possible for me to organise that."

Abhishek got very angry. He was very much against dowry, but he also realised there was very little option. He said to Vivek: "Organise the marriage and I will arrange the dowry."

Vivek said: "That's very nice of you but it has to be low-key because my savings are running out. I cannot spend a lot of money."

Abhishek reassured him: "Don't worry. We are here."

A couple of months later, the young daughter got married and she went to live in Alipore in a decent house with her husband.

Vivek was very pleased and relieved. He had taken care of two big responsibilities; his two daughters were married and he had very decent sons-in-law.

He still had to look after his young son, who was still in school, but Abhishek had promised that he would look after his education. Another good thing was that Chandan liked Abhishek very much.

CHAPTER 19

Abhishek and Sharmila were very busy decorating their house and getting all the beds and furniture. Abhishek was extremely busy at work but he loved his job. Indian Chemical was getting bigger every day and, as it was expanding, Abhishek had the power to employ a lot of people, mainly builders, painters, machine tool operators, engineers and office staff. By now the company employed nearly 5,000 people.

There were many managers and assistant managers under Abhishek. He had appointed a smart young man called Abbas Rauf as his personal assistant. He spoke English, Hindi and Bengali fluently and soon became a right-hand man to Abhishek.

On the factory floor, Abhishek told his managers to employ Muslims and Hindus equally to ensure harmony. He felt it was imperative that equal opportunities were given to both communities, even though at that time Muslims made up only 17 per cent of the population of Calcutta.

His cricketing role was also getting busier but he had a secretary who covered all day-to-day activities. Abhishek went to the office only once a week, and when there was a meeting.

Life was going well but by the end of the 1930s the shadow of the Second World War was looming over India. India, as the biggest and richest colony in the British Empire, had become a prime target. Lots of Indians were mobilised and sent to Europe to fight the Germans - it is estimated about one million Indians joined the Allies.

But in India the fear was that the Japanese might attack the country. It would be easy to attack Calcutta, the capital of Bengal, via Burma. Abhishek had to do compulsory army training - so he did army, First Aid and fire brigade training. One day in training he had to jump from the second floor. He was supposed to land on a net, but somebody dropped the net and Abhishek hurt his back.

The doctor said he might have a stress fracture of the spine and he was kept in bed rest for six weeks. Following that, he had extensive physio and massage, but Abhishek continued to do his work.

There was more bad news when rioting engulfed Bengal again. This time Abhishek's younger two maternal uncles, Anup and Akash, left home and turned up with their families at Abhishek's house. Abhishek had to welcome them.

Through one of his contacts he found out that one of the Muslim landlords from Midnapur in West Bengal wanted to exchange his land with property in the east and the Government was encouraging it. Akash was very lucky. He got an exchange with Mr Basira Ahmed and it went well. After a few weeks, with all his family and his papers, he shifted to Midnapur and took up farming.

Getting a job for Anup was much more difficult but again, through a cricketing friend, Abhishek organised a role for him in the newly built Tata Steel plant in Jamshedpur in Bihar. Anup was very reluctant to go but, after several months of unemployment, he felt he had no choice but to accept it. Narayan was in two minds at this stage whether to leave his ancestors' land or soldier on and hope things got better. For the time being, Narayan decided to stay put.

A year later, Abhishek and Sharmila's first son was born at home. They called him Soumitra Banerjee. The boy was like his mother, very fair. Tarini was delighted and sent sweets to everybody in the locality.

But unfortunately, war had broken out. There was a curfew everywhere, and a huge food shortage. The Japanese started bombing indiscriminately over Calcutta and the surrounding area. Abhishek became extremely busy, not only in his job but in vigilante activities in the evening and night.

One night, a Japanese bomb landed within 100 yards of Abhishek's house, leaving a huge crater. The rumour was that the Japanese would bomb more and more until the Allied forces surrendered. Abhishek came home and asked Sharmila and Tarini to take Soumitra and all the toys. Sharmila asked: "Where are we going?"

Abhishek said: "It is not safe any more to stay in Calcutta. I have spoken to uncle Akash on a trunk call. I will take you there to stay and will bring you back as soon as the bombing finishes."

Abhishek put them in his official car with the driver and they drove straight to Midnapur. It was a four-hour drive on a bumpy road. Akash was waiting for them and Abhishek told him that as soon as the bombing stopped he would come back to take them. He gave Akash 500 rupees and Akash said: "That is a lot of money." Abhishek said: "Don't worry. Leave it for the time being."

People in Calcutta were now very frightened. Very few people were on the street and there was a curfew. The situation was pretty miserable.

One evening Abhishek came home a bit early and saw from afar a family was sitting on the steps of his house. When he came near, he couldn't believe his eyes. It was uncle Narayan and his whole family. They had been driven off their ancestors' land and they had nowhere to go. The only address they had was Abhishek's.

There was nothing anyone could do. Abhishek was, like millions of other Hindus and Muslims, simply helpless. Everybody knew it was not right but nobody had stood up to stop it. People of a very peaceful, docile country had suddenly become violent towards their brothers and sisters.

Narayan had some money and jewellery and he had experience of running a big business. Again, after a couple of weeks, Abhishek could organise a supervisor's job in a factory outside Calcutta for Narayan. He and his family soon moved out to a rented property near his job.

Abhishek thought, that's what fate is like. Narayan, who was one of the biggest landowners in the state, was now working as a supervisor in a shoe factory on a small salary. At least he and his family were safe.

The momentum of Quit India had started gaining pace. The Congress

Party, the biggest party in India at the time, had mobilised the whole country to campaign for the British to leave.

At the same time, some Muslims were insistent they should have a land of their own. Basically, they wanted the country to be divided along religious lines. But most Hindus and Muslims were against that.

Gandhi had started his non-violent movement but his authority, after in-fighting in the Congress Party, had diminished in such a way that it seemed things were out of his control. Even Hindu nationalists were very much against his policies of appeasement of Muslims - so much so that they started their own political party called Jana Sangh.

But Jawaharlal Nehru was keen to become the Prime Minister of an independent India. He was eager to keep hold of Kashmir, which was his ancestors' birthplace, and in return allowed Punjab and Bengal to be divided.

PART FIVE

CHAPTER 20

1943 was a landmark year in the history of Bengal and India. Against the backdrop of the Quit India movement, with high tension and religious rioting, Bengal was in a very bad shape.

On top of that, for two consecutive seasons it rained like hell. There was flooding all over the state. Two sets of crops were demolished and ruined, leading to extreme food shortages. Rationing started. Poor people were dying on the streets, crying out for one bowl of rice.

Abhishek discussed the famine with his board of directors and started a kitchen in one of the factory grounds. Before dawn, thousands of people were queuing. There were ladies with malnourished children in their lap, others who could hardly walk - the suffering of the people was unimaginable. Indian Chemical's kitchen tried to feed people at least one meal, mostly rice and lentils.

The Government asked the British Government for urgent help and food supplies. The Australian Government was kind enough to send two large ships full of rice and wheat towards Calcutta. But the British Prime Minister, Winston Churchill, had different views. He diverted both the ships towards Liverpool, saying the food was needed more in England than India.

The consequences for Bengal were catastrophic. Nearly two million people died of starvation in the Bengal famine - more than the total number of deaths on the Western Front in World War One. People looked like skeletons covered by skin.

The famine had a huge effect on Abhishek's life. Evening after evening, he sat alone in his office wondering why it had happened and how it had not been stopped.

Because of the turbulence, the Chief Executive of Indian Chemical decided to go back to England. Although he loved the city and its people, the political unrest made him decide it was high time to go back. Abhishek applied for the job and was selected.

Although he was still a young man, he was now CEO of one of the biggest companies in the state and also had a place in the boardroom. Everybody had huge expectations of him, both at the company and also in his social circle. Now he was extremely busy. His day started early in the morning and finished after eight o' clock in the evening. Also, because his company was expanding and creating many jobs, it became known that he could employ people.

From early morning men, women and children used to queue up outside his house with folded hands. There was an iron gate and a security guard keeping people under control, but Abhishek always had time for these people. He used to stop and talk to each and every one and see if he could help. Even if he couldn't give them a job, he knew that these people were very honest. He would ask a servant to give them food or some money.

After work, he would see how the charity feeding centre was getting on. He would ask all his acquaintances to donate something to it. An English guy called Joseph, who used to be an English teacher, volunteered to be in charge of the feeding centre. Joseph and his Indian wife were working day and night. Also, on behalf of Abhishek, Himanshu and Bishwanath's son turned up to help. Joseph did the day-to-day running and gave the account to Abhishek.

Abhishek's life was getting very disrupted with all these people asking for help. There was a limit - how much can one individual do? Sharmila didn't mind the philanthropic work he did, but Tarini was getting very anxious that Abhishek was working too hard and people were exploiting him. Abhishek would laugh and tell his mum: "These people are in desperate need. Somebody has to help them. If I don't, who will?"

Abhishek would get up in the morning, have breakfast and leave home. He didn't take lunch and when he came back home he would take a shower, change and go first to Tarini's room and ask how her day had been. What had she eaten? How was she feeling?

Tarini would tell him who had come to the house and what they were looking for. She would say nice things about Sharmila because they got on very well. Tarini wanted to have a festival and feast to celebrate their son's first birthday but Abhishek said: "No. There is a famine going on in the country. We can't have a celebration."

Sunday was a relaxing day for Abhishek. He would go to watch cricket on the Calcutta *Maidan*. Some days Sharmila came with him and after the match they would go to Esplanade to a cinema, have dinner and come home late. Tarini liked that. She thought Abhishek worked very hard, so he should relax.

It was becoming increasingly obvious that the British were leaving India. It was no longer a question of how, but when. They wanted to leave peacefully but they knew the country would be divided - everybody knew there could be a bloodbath.

A new Viceroy was sent to negotiate with Hindus and Muslims for a peaceful resolution. They decided that part of Punjab, part of Bengal and all of Sindh would form a newly created Pakistan, but Kashmir remained a thorny issue. The British Government appointed two professors from Oxford to decide how the land would be divided.

These professors had never been to India. It was sad and ironic that people sitting in London decided the fate of the country by partition.

Gandhi frequently said that he was opposed to partition and even declared that Bengal will be divided over his dead body.

The thugs and extremists on both sides were having a field day and they took full advantage of people's uncertainty and fear. Abhishek was sitting in his office when one of his employees, who happened to be a Hindu nationalist, told him some terrorists were planning to attack the Muslim employees on their way home after the night shift in revenge for a riot in Dhaka the previous week.

Abhishek couldn't sit and do nothing. He called his PA Rauf, went to the factory and looked at the list of the names coming for the next shift. He picked out who were the Muslims among them. He gave those names to one of the security guards, Ratan, and said: "With two guards, go to the places these people live and tell them that I have told them not to come to work. Stay at home."

Then he found out how many people still in the factory were Muslims. There were 65 of them. He told them to come to the canteen and have breakfast but not to go out of the factory.

He went to the Police Commissioner's office with Rauf and told him what the information was. The commissioner, with a large number of officers, came with Abhishek to the factory. Abhishek called all the Hindu employees to close the factory for the day and they formed a cordon around the Muslim brothers, with police around them, and took them slowly to Kamarhati station and dropped each of them at their house. The fundamentalists' whole plan was completely foiled.

Abhishek, however, became the target of Hindu fundamentalists. One of the Hindu leaders told Abhishek that he was behaving like a traitor. "We need to teach these Muslims some lessons, otherwise they won't stop killing and raping our Hindu mothers and sisters," he said.

Abhishek said: "I am not frightened of you or your thugs. You may not know my background. My ancestral home has been burned down by some Muslim thugs. But I can't kill some innocent Muslim guys just for the sake of revenge."

A few months later, Abhishek became Chairman of the Calcutta Cricket Board. Lots of sports people came to him for help.

On August 15 1947, India got its independence at last. It led to one of the bloodiest partitions of any country in human history. The estimates of the number of people killed range between 200,000 and two million. It was one of the darkest and most shameful parts of Indian history. Just because of religion, people killed each other.

Women from both sides were raped and tortured, and millions were uprooted from their ancestral homelands. One of the by-products was large-scale starvation. It was a haunting time. Those who lived in India and Pakistan felt a sense of guilt, a sense of helplessness.

In the middle of all this mayhem, many people showed their kindness and generosity. There were many millions of families like Abhishek's scattered all over Bengal, Punjab and Sindh.

Abbas Rauf and his family were scared to stay in Calcutta. Abhishek was also worried for him. Through a connection of his family, Rauf got a job in the newly formed East Pakistan radio station in Dhaka, but he was part of Abhishek's life. It was a very difficult decision and he was scared to travel to Dhaka because of the frequent killings on the trains.

Abhishek said he would take them and drop them at the border. So Rauf and his wife, with a few belongings, went in Abhishek's car one night. They drove to Bongaon, on the border with East Pakistan, and gave a bribe to the police, who allowed them to enter East Pakistan. Rauf was crying and looking back. Abhishek embraced him and said: "I am sure you will do well and I will meet you again some time."

Abhishek's driver Mohammed Mia was missing for three months. Nobody knew where he had disappeared to. He was from Bihar and a very good-looking young Muslim man. Because of partition, everybody took it for granted that he had gone to East Pakistan or back to Bihar.

One fine Sunday morning, Abhishek was reading a paper when suddenly a young man with his young wife came and touched his feet. Abhishek couldn't believe it and he said: "Where have you been all this time?"

Mo told the perplexed Abhishek: "Sir, this is my wife Sita. Please call me Radheshyam."

Abhishek said: "What exactly is happening?"

Radheshyam said: "At the height of the riot, I was ambushed and I was going to get killed by a Hindu mob. Our other factory driver, Basudevji, saved my and my wife's life saying, 'He is Radheshyam and he lives with me, leave him alone'.

"I got married in a temple to his daughter – so I am now Radheshyam and Sita is my wife. He protected me and my wife and I owe my life to him."

CHAPTER 21

India had its independence, but at what cost? Millions died in the religious fighting. Millions died from starvation. And millions were uprooted and politically cleansed from their homeland.

The biggest impact was felt by Bengal and Punjab, and partly by Sindh. Pakistan was in two parts on either side of India. West Pakistan basically consisted of Punjab, Sindh and Baluch, and East Pakistan had been created by the partition of Bengal.

Sikhs and Hindus were driven out of Punjab. Even the holy temple of *Guru Nanak*, the founder of Sikhism, was not spared. East Pakistan was smaller and Dhaka became its capital. Trainloads of people moved from one end to the other.

India was left with 16 provinces, but the Kashmir issue was fudged. Constitutionally, it was given special status, with more autonomy and more economic support from the centre, because Kashmir was the only Muslim majority state. So part of Kashmir was taken over by Pakistan and called Azad Kashmir.

The Brahmin *pandits* from Kashmir became landless and were driven out. Pakistan got its independence but, because of the war and factional fighting, the country was broke. Both India and Pakistan needed new direction and leadership for rebuilding.

India had Jawaharlal Nehru as its first Prime Minister from the Congress Party, while Pakistan was led by the Muslim league and Muhammad Jinnah.

Millions of Muslims decided to stay in India. Eighty-five per cent of the population were Hindus, but the Indian Government declared it a secular state. The East Pakistan population was supported by lots of Muslims from Bengal and Bihar, who went to East Pakistan. Delhi was India's capital, while Pakistan had Rawalpindi as its first capital. From there it ruled East Pakistan, while Dhaka remained the local capital for East Bengal.

The British, after ruling India for nearly 300 years, left hurriedly. Their arrival had spelled the end of the Mughal Empire. Where they had once ruled most of India, fighting among themselves reduced their grip. Siraj ud-Daulah was the last independent *Nawab* of Bengal and the British, by cleverly supporting his brother-in-law, Mir Jafar, ended the rule of Mughal Empire.

They started off ruling by proxy Mir Jafar and, after him, Mir Qasim. Then the East India Company slowly took over the rest of the country. The British learned the country's mood very well. Before they arrived, India had been conquered and ruled by many tribal groups like Mughals.

But the British did not do that. Slowly and patiently, through business and the economy, took over the running of the country. Having started as a trading company, they became rulers.

They did a lot of good things. They organised the printing of books and restructured the education system. India had a very rich educational heritage but it needed modernising, which the British did. They built roads and railway systems that connected one end of the country to the other.

They also created water and sewage systems in the big cities and managed to introduce electricity there. All the manual work was done by Indians, the supervisors were Indians - but the bosses were all British.

By doing all this, they made a hefty profit. When the British Empire spanned the globe, India was the jewel in the crown. Men like Clive and Hastings ruled India and when they went back to England they were very wealthy and became lords of the land.

Their tactic for running the country was to divide and rule. The British conquered about 65 countries around the world and they ran them using the Indian model. They took lots of Indians from different parts of India to other colonial lands for building houses, laying railways, building roads and transport and also planting sugarcane and cotton. They produced huge profits at the expense of poor Indians working hard in these countries.

During the last part of British rule, about 42,000 British personnel used to live in Calcutta alone. They were in top jobs like judges, police officers, civil servants and top hospital doctors. In Britain there was a huge competition among civil servants to get a posting to India.

Many of the British stayed in India after retirement, married local girls and produced a sizable Anglo-Indian community. Calcutta became a hub of a large number of churches scattered all over the city.

CHAPTER 22

By 1950, Abhishek had become more powerful than before. Not only was he a director of Indian Chemical, he was also Chairman of the Calcutta Cricket Board and a member of the Indian Hockey Association. It was difficult to manage the balance between family life and his hectic workload but Abhishek didn't complain.

Things were much calmer now although a large number of refugees were still pouring across the borders in both directions.

Because of his multiple activities, Abhishek had to throw many parties. For a friendly or small gathering, he hosted at home with Sharmila helping out, but for corporate events he mostly used the Grand Hotel, a five-star venue in the centre of Calcutta. He always invited some Indian musicians - classical, vocal or instrumental. These parties were very popular and Abhishek was a very good after-dinner speaker.

He spent more time in his office and visited the factory only once in a while. He was sitting in his office one day when his secretary brought all the post and in among the correspondence was a gift card. Abhishek quickly opened it and saw the sender's name - it was from Abbas Rauf in Dhaka. He had written to inform Abhishek he was doing well with his wife and had got a job in the news desk covering current affairs in East Pakistan. Abhishek was delighted for Abbas, immediately dictated a letter and told his secretary to post it the same day.

Calcutta was getting very crowded nowadays. Every day, thousands of people were pouring in from East Bengal with their luggage, their tin boxes and a few belongings like beds and bedding. In some places they had taken over empty land and put up tarpaulin huts for their families. The local people didn't like it - so there was increasing friction.

Some people started staying in the stations, particularly Sealdah, where platform nine had become a sleeping ground for these refugees. They had taken over the footpaths of Calcutta. One could hardly walk.

The local government tried to move them out and the central government offered a place called Dandakaranya, in Madhya Pradesh, a huge jungle in the middle of nowhere, for these refugees to settle. Few accepted the offer and took a train there. Most of them decided to stay on the platforms and footpaths or force their way on to other people's property.

One Monday morning in 1952, Abhishek was in the back seat of his car on his way to the office. Radheshyam was driving and his secretary was sitting next to the driver. The car pulled up in front of the office. It was a huge building with six floors and 10 steps up to the building. Radheshyam stopped the car and came out to open the door for Abhishek.

An elderly man with a stick, wearing a dirty *dhoti* and a torn vest, unshaven and with folded hands, was standing outside the car. As Abhishek stepped out, the old man said: "Sir, can I talk to you for a second?"

Radheshyam and the secretary moved the man aside and said: "Move, move, let *Sahib* go."

These things happened with Abhishek all the time but he felt bad about the way the man had been pushed. He said: "That's fine. Tell me what you want to say."

The man dropped a bombshell. He said: "Sir, my name is Rabi Guha. I am from your father's village and I knew him well."

Abhishek leaned forward with disbelief and said: "What did you say? You say you knew my father?"

"Yes, I did."

Abhishek said to the man: "Get in the car."

So, the man sat next to him in the car and Abhishek said to his secretary: "I was supposed to have a meeting at 11.00. Cancel that and reschedule it. Tell them I have got urgent business to sort out. If anything is urgent, give me a call. I will be at home."

Radheshyam knew Abhishek very well. He said: "Shall we go home then?"

"Yes," said Abhishek. When they arrived home he said to Mr Guha: "Come with me."

He called his servant Sankar and said: "Take this man, give him a shower and give him a new *dhoti* and shirt. Then he said to Sharmila: "This poor guy has not eaten for some days. Can you ask the cook to make a good lunch for me to have with him?"

Rabi couldn't believe the treatment he was receiving. They had a big lunch and Rabi ate well.

Abhishek took him to his study, closed the door and said: "Have a seat. You said you knew my father. So, tell me how you knew him and what you knew about him."

Rabi said: "I used to be a farmer in Dhruba Banerjee's farm."

Abhishek said: "Dhruba Banerjee, my father's uncle?"

Rabi said: "Yes. We have been working on your ancestors' farm for generations. So I knew Ashok very well. He was a lovely man, a very intelligent and clever man. Whenever we had any problem, we used to go to him. You should be proud that your father was a very well-liked man but unfortunately, he passed away very young.

"When the first riot broke out, we had nowhere to go. We decided to stay, hoping things would get better. Unfortunately, it got worse and worse and recently one Hindu girl was raped in our village and we were the only two Hindu families left.

"One Muslim friend wanted to buy my house and that was the only thing I had, so I sold it, maybe for a quarter of what it was worth, and left with my wife and two sons. Apart from a few clothes, we couldn't bring anything with us."

Abhishek said: "Where are you staying then?"

Rabi said: "I am staying on platform seven. My sons put up a tarpaulin tent, we sleep inside and my sons sleep outside."

Abhishek asked: "How old are your sons?"

"Twenty and 18."

Abhishek said: "What are they doing now?"

Rabi, with folded hands, said: "They need some work. Somebody showed me your picture in a newspaper and someone said you were from Bikrampur. You look exactly like your father, so I knew it had to be you. I was standing outside your office for the last seven days."

Abhishek said: "Why didn't you tell me then?"

Rabi said: "You are always with lots of people and the security guard won't let me come near you. But today it was my lucky day."

Abhishek took a piece of paper and said: "What's your eldest son's name?"

"Sarat Gruha."

Abhishek wrote in his pad: "Dear Himanshu, please organise this lad a job, any job. That's my personal request. Yours, Abhishek."

He put the letter in an envelope, wrote Himanshu's address and told Rabi: "Ask your son to take this letter to this gentleman, he will get a job tomorrow."

Then he gave Rabi 100 rupees and said: "I don't want you to sleep on a railway platform with your wife. With this money you will definitely get a room somewhere in Calcutta."

Rabi, with folded hands, cried and said: "I believe in God. You are just God to my family."

Abhishek said: "Before you go, one last question. Do you know anything about my father's remaining family, aunt Radha and my uncle Adi?"

Rabi sat down again and said: "As far as I know, Radha's family did exchange land and went somewhere in West Bengal, but I don't know exactly where they have gone."

Then Rabi paused for a few seconds. Abhishek said: "But what?"

"About Adi," said Rabi, "I can only tell you what I heard from rumours. When the riot was at its peak, when everyone was killing everyone and burning everything, Adi was hiding in Abdul Mia's house with his family.

"Unfortunately, Abdul Mia was killed in the riot. After a month or so, when things slightly calmed down, Abdul's wife Mumtaz and their daughter and Aditya all put on burkhas to hide and they went to, as far I heard, Mumtaz's brother's house in Dhaka.

"Mumtaz's brother had a thriving business in the export and import of garments. Since independence they got huge contracts everywhere. What happened to Adi since then, I honestly don't know.

"I followed the business of Rasul, but he is not running the business now. The gentleman who heads the company is called Habib Islam. He is very well known in East Bengal because he employs a huge number of people.

"As Habib Islam is the man who runs Mumtaz's brother's business - and Adi went to stay with them - he must know something about Aditya."

Abhishek immediately took a pen and paper and wrote down: "Habib Islam… import-export business… man from Dhaka to trace."

CHAPTER 23

Abhishek was upset for a few days. He sat in his office and wondered how to trace Habib Islam. Suddenly he remembered the card from Abbas Rauf. He took it out - and Abbas's telephone number was written there.

Abhishek asked the operator: "Could you connect me to a number in Dhaka?"

The operator said: "Yes, sir."

The phone rang and a lady picked up and said: "Radio controller's office."

"May I talk to Mr Abbas Rauf?"

"May I know who you are and what this relates to?"

Abhishek said politely: "I am ringing from Calcutta. My name is Abhishek Banerjee and I am a friend of Mr Rauf."

He could hear the lady saying to someone that there was a Mr Banerjee from Calcutta who wanted to talk to him, and did he want to take the call?

Immediately, Abhishek could hear Abbas's voice saying: "Sir, is that you? It's such a pleasure to hear your voice. How is the family?"

Abhishek said: "Fine. What are you doing now?"

Abbas said: "With your blessing, I am the controller of state radio for news and current affairs."

Abhishek said: "Abbas, I need a favour from you."

Abbas said: "Don't ask. Just order me."

Abhishek said: "I want to meet a man called Habib Islam. He is an import and export businessman."

Abbas interrupted and said: "Sir, everybody knows him. He is huge. He is very successful and he is one of the top businessmen in our country. I interviewed him once. He is in his mid-60s, a very polite and very handsome man. He lives in one of the posh parts of Dhaka. If you want, I can find out more about him and give you a call next week."

Abhishek was very anxious and impatient all week. Abbas rang back and said he had tried to organise an appointment with Mr Islam but his office declined, saying that he was very busy at the present time. He was not meeting people or giving interviews.

Abbas said: "One option you could take is to arrive at his house randomly and see if you could talk to him - but it could be a wasted journey if he doesn't talk."

Abhishek said: "If I come, Abbas, can you help me?"

"Of course, I will do whatever I can. But why do you want to see this man so badly?"

Abhishek replied: "I can only tell you once I meet him."

Every day there were two flights from Calcutta to Dhaka. One went at 10 o'clock in the morning and the same plane returned that night.

Abhishek asked his secretary to book a day-return to Dhaka. He rang and gave the details of the flight to Abbas, who said he would be at the airport with his car. So, the purpose of the journey was business. Abbas also said he had taken the day off so that he could spend more time with Abhishek.

At home, Tarini was very concerned when she heard that Abhishek was going to Dhaka. She said to him: "Why do you want to go to Dhaka now? Ask someone else to go in your place."

But Abhishek said: "No, this is so important. I can't leave it to other people." Sharmila guessed that he was on a mission.

Abhishek put on a black suit and red tie and put a few things in a black briefcase. He had a seat in executive class. For once he looked very tense. It took two hours to arrive at Dhaka airport. When he came out, Abbas Rauf was standing at the gate.

Abbas had put on a lot of weight and had glasses on. They got to his car and Abbas drove him around and stopped in front of a restaurant. They had a cup of tea and Abbas told Abhishek he couldn't get an appointment but they would still take a chance and see if they could meet Mr Islam.

Abbas drove to the posh part of Dhaka and stopped in front of a very large house with an iron gate and a brick wall surrounding the house. There was a pebble pavement from the gate to the house and a few smart cars parked around. Abbas looked at Abhishek and said: "This is Mr Islam's house."

There was a big golden plaque outside the main gate bearing the name Habib Islam. Abbas parked the car and Abhishek said: "It looks like Buckingham Palace."

Both approached the gate. A security guard stopped them. Abbas said: "We are from Dhaka radio station."

The guard said: "Have you got an appointment?"

Abbas said: "Sort of."

"In that case," said the guard, "come inside and sit in his guest room and talk to his secretary in the house."

Abbas and Abhishek entered a cool large room with walls full of pictures of Islam receiving awards at home and abroad. A young, good-looking lady with a beautiful *sari* said to Abbas: "I am Mr Islam's secretary. I can't see any appointment you made before but I will go and ask Sir whether he will talk to you."

After a few minutes of waiting anxiously, she came back and said: "I have spoken to Sir and I am sorry, he is extremely busy today. The German business delegates are coming to his office, so within five minutes he will leave home. But if you make an appointment, he is happy to give you an interview next week."

Abhishek got despondent that everyone thought that he had come to conduct an interview, but he told Abbas: "I am not going away without talking to him."

The house was very large but outside there was a rectangular space covered with pebble stones, with a few tall trees around it. It was protected by a tall wall and two iron gates, one for going out and one for coming in.

Abhishek came out of the office and said: "It seems he is going out very soon. The driver is cleaning a big Mercedes. As soon as he comes out, I will go forward and talk to him."

Abbas said: "That's not a bad idea. But the security people might throw us out." So they stood in the corner and waited. Abhishek tied his tie knot again.

After about 10 minutes, a very tall gentleman in his mid-60s wearing a blue three-piece suit, white shirt and a blue tie and a beard, with very polished shoes, walked out of the house door towards the Mercedes. There were three people walking behind him with bags and files.

Abhishek said: "Let's go."

Mr Islam's driver opened the door of the car and was standing there when Abbas came and put his hand forward to shake hands. Mr Islam shook hands and Abbas said: "Mr Islam, I am Mr Rauf, controller of the radio station."

Mr Islam said: "Glad to meet you Mr Rauf, but I have got a very important meeting with some German people in my office. Today you have to excuse me."

He was about to sit in his car when Abbas said: "It's not me, Mr Islam. It's my friend, who came from Calcutta and would like to talk to you."

By now Islam's driver had closed the door. Mr Islam pulled the window down and said: "What did you say?"

So far Abhishek had been very quiet. He was in awe of this successful handsome man. Mr Islam said: "Please make an appointment with my secretary. I will definitely talk to him."

But this time Abhishek said firmly: "Mr Islam, my name is Abhishek Banerjee and my father's name was Ashok Banerjee."

Mr Islam told his driver to stop the car. He leaned forward and said: "You are the son of Ashok Banerjee from Sukhobaspur?" He got out of the car and hugged Abhishek very firmly for a long time. Tears were rolling down from his eyes. The people around couldn't believe what was going on.

He composed himself and told his assistant: "You guys go ahead to the office and ask Mr Rahman, the CEO, to do the discussion. I won't be able to come today."

And he called to another gentleman: "Mr Ghafoor, would you be kind enough to take Mr Rauf with you and look after him."

Mr Islam put his arms around Abhishek's shoulders and said: "Come on, make yourself at home. What do you do?"

Abhishek said: "I am CEO of Indian Chemical."

Mr Islam said: "That's excellent. I do a lot of business with your company."

Someone opened the main door and they came into a big sitting room. Mr Islam took his jacket and tie off and said to Abhishek: "Sit down and relax. I will call my wife Jahanara, who will be very pleased to see you." It was a very large and well-decorated sitting room.

Mr Islam asked Abhishek: "Are you here for business? "

Abhishek said: "No, no - I am here for a day just to meet you."

Mr Islam gave a big sigh and said: "Maybe both of us left it too late." Abhishek nodded his head. "How do you know Mr Rauf?"

"He used to be my PA. Through an intermediary I came to know your address and someone told me that you might know something about my family."

Mr Islam became completely quiet. He stood up and looked outside the window. His eyes were moist. He wiped his eyes and said: "What you want to know?"

Abhishek said: "I wanted to know what happened to my father's brother Aditya. My father, while he was alive, looked for him everywhere. He died at the age of 33 with a sense of guilt that he let his brother down."

Mr Islam again looked at the corner of the room and outside. The tears were rolling down his face and he said in a whispering voice: "I am very sorry, Abhishek – I can't help you there. I do not know what happened to your uncle Aditya."

He took his handkerchief out and sobbed for a minute, then said: "One thing I can tell you. You must be proud of your father. He was the best man I have ever met in my entire life, but that was a previous life and a different life."

Mr Islam excused himself and left the room. After a few minutes, he came back again holding the hands of his wife Jahanara. He said to her: "This is Abhishek, Ashok-da's son. Abhishek, this is your aunt Jahanara."

Abhishek touched Jahanara's feet. Mr Islam said: "He looks and behaves exactly like his dad. Abhishek, stay and have dinner with us and stay tonight. I need to talk to you."

Abhishek said: "No sir, I have a return ticket for this evening."

"Don't worry, give it to me. I will change it."

"I have lots of work back home. I need to go."

"Go tomorrow."

Now fully composed, Mr Islam called Mr Rauf and said: "Your friend is going to stay with us tonight and I promise to give you an interview any time next week." Abbas felt completely confused, so he said goodbye to everybody and left.

Jahanara cooked a huge, excellent meal. Mr Islam and Abhishek spoke till late in the night. The next day, Mr Islam said: "I will take you to the airport." He knew everybody at the airport, and they allowed him across the tarmac to the foot of the staircase to the plane.

They embraced each other and Abhishek touched Mr Islam's feet. Mr Islam said: "You don't know how much happiness and pleasure I got meeting you."

Abhishek said: "It was a dream come true."

Both wiped their tears. Mr Islam said: "I will be here if you come back, but don't look for Adi. You won't find him."

Abhishek got on the plane and sat next to the window. The evening sun over Dhaka was red. It was still hot but the sun was slowly going down. There was a faint rainbow in the sky on the other side. Far away he could see the paddy fields moving in a gentle breeze.

He could see Mr Islam, a successful businessman, standing on the tarmac wiping his tears from his eyes. The plane engine started and Abhishek looked again.

It was take-off time. He looked at what had been the land of his ancestors for generations and many, many years. They were no more, but at least Mr Islam was there.

The pilot started the engine. Each and every passenger was sat in the seats and a quiet hum of excitement and expectation hung heavy in the air.

Abhishek sat quietly in his chair, closed his eyes. He had the vague awareness that the air hostess had started explaining what to do and what not to do in case of an emergency.

The plane started taxiing. Abhishek was thinking. Thinking about his father. He thought that, while he could not remember his father, he had seen a lot of photos of his father.

As the plane took off, Abhishek's eyes started to close. As he drifted into a restful sleep, the image in front of his eyes was that of his father's face. He felt at peace.

He felt a sense of gratitude.

ABOUT THE AUTHOR

In *A Sense Of Gratitude*, Biren Banerjee celebrates the lives of his ancestors in an India that is long past but that echoes strongly in the modern world. He depicts vividly the realities of 19th-century village life in Bengal, the bustle of Kolkata at the opening of the 20th centuty – and the tension and anguish of Partition.

Biren Banerjee is a respected orthopaedic surgeon based in Birmingham, who has always enjoyed reading, learning and travelling the world.

Born in India, he has spent most of his working life in England. His wife is also a doctor. He has two grown-up sons, one living in London and the other in the United States.